NIGHTBOOKS

J. A. White

NIGHTBOOKS

Katherine Tegen Books is an imprint of HarperCollins Publishers.

Nightbooks
 For information address HarperCollins Children's Books, a division of HarperCollins Publishers, 195 Broadway, New York, NY 10007.
www.harpercollinschildrens.com

Library of Congress Control Number: 2017954128
ISBN 978-0-06-256008-7

Typography by Amy Ryan
19 20 21 22 CG/LSCH 10 9 8 7
❖

First Edition

For Jack Paccione Jr.—
partner in imagination

CONTENTS

I

THE WRONG FLOOR

After his family had finally fallen asleep, Alex slung the backpack over his shoulder and snuck out of the apartment, easing the front door gently home so it didn't slam shut. The eighth-floor hallway looked drearier than ever without any sunlight coming through its small windows. Alex lingered on the doormat, fighting the urge to return to his warm, comfortable bed.

If you do that, he thought, *you'll still be the same old Alex Mosher tomorrow.*

Weirdo.

Freak.

Loser.

Is that what you want?

"No," he whispered.

Before he could change his mind, Alex started toward

the elevator at the end of the hall.

During the day, snippets of his neighbors' lives leaked through the thin doors: muffled conversations, the loud blare of televisions, Ms. Garcia's son practicing his violin. At this time of night, however, the hallway was nearly silent. The only sounds were a grimy lightbulb that buzzed like an angry hornet and a soft rustling from Alex's backpack, as though its contents were struggling to escape their fate.

Sorry, Alex thought, feeling a wave of guilt. *I wish I didn't have to do this. But it's better this way.*

He reached the elevator and pressed the Down button on the cracked panel. Far below him, ancient gears squealed away the silence. Alex winced and peeked over his shoulder, hoping that the sound didn't wake any of his neighbors. The stairs would have been a quieter option, but Alex wanted to reach his destination as quickly as possible so he didn't have an opportunity to second-guess his decision.

Ding!

The elevator doors jerked open with a pained squeak. Smudged mirrors paneled the walls.

Alex stepped inside and clicked the *B* button.

The basement was his favorite place in the entire apartment building. It was spooky and weird and packed ceiling-high with towers of knickknacks left behind by former tenants, like a graveyard for unwanted items. The most amazing part, however, was the boiler, an iron monster built nearly sixty years ago. Alex called it Old Smokey.

It was his destination tonight.

The elevator doors closed, and the car began to descend in slow, jerky increments. Alex tapped his foot impatiently. Though his backpack was far lighter than usual, it seemed to weigh him down like an anchor.

I'll feel better after they're gone, he thought. *Just toss them in the flames and walk away. Don't even stick around to watch them burn.*

Of course, Alex could have just dumped the contents of his backpack down the trash chute and been done with it, but that seemed cruel. Cremating them in Old Smokey felt more honorable, like setting the body of a fallen warrior aflame. Alex figured he owed them a good death, at least. After all, he was the one who had created them.

The elevator stopped. The doors creaked open.

Alex tilted his head in confusion.

Instead of the basement, an unfamiliar hallway stretched out before him. He checked the digital display at the top of the elevator: 4. *Must be broken,* he thought, jabbing the *B* button with his index finger. The elevator didn't move.

Alex sighed with frustration.

Looks like I'm taking the stairs after all, he thought.

He stepped off the elevator and headed toward the stairwell. The fourth floor had the same basic layout as the eighth, but it was noticeably darker. Alex glanced up at the lightbulbs, wondering if a few of them had burned out, but they seemed to be working fine. For some strange reason, however, their glow didn't radiate as far as it should, as though the darkness of this particular hallway was harder to penetrate than the ordinary kind.

Just my crazy imagination, Alex thought, ignoring the cold sensation creeping down his spine. *The bulbs are probably just old or—*

He heard voices.

They were coming from the apartment at the end of the hall. At first, Alex thought it was just the people who lived there. As he got closer, however, creepy music rose in the background, and Alex realized that the voices belonged to characters from a movie. He broke into a big grin as he recognized the dialogue.

That's Night of the Living Dead*!* he thought.

Alex had been four years old the first time he saw the movie. He was supposed to have been asleep, but the strange sounds coming from the living room had piqued his curiosity, and so he had crept out of bed to investigate. His mom and dad were cuddled up on the couch, sharing a bowl of popcorn. Alex hid behind his dad's easy chair and trained his eyes on the television.

He had never been so terrified—or exhilarated—in his life.

By the time that his parents realized they had an unwelcome visitor, it was too late. Alex was in love. At the end of the month, his Thomas trains had been exiled to a bin in the basement, replaced by toy monsters, plastic fangs, and a stuffed ghost named Boo. He dismantled his Lego fire trucks and rocket ships and used the bricks to build a haunted house. At the library, Alex insisted on borrowing only the picture books with little Halloween labels on their spines, despite the fact that it was June.

Night of the Living Dead had been his introduction to the world of creepy things, and for that reason it held a special place in his heart. Hearing it now, an overpowering desire to watch the movie again fogged all other thoughts. Alex approached the door of apartment 4E, the static-filled soundtrack reeling him in like a fishing line, and pressed his ear against it. It was one of the earliest scenes in the movie, just before Barbara and her brother are attacked by a zombie at the graveyard.

I've barely missed anything at all, Alex thought with excitement. He had, for the moment, completely forgotten about his backpack and his reason for coming out tonight. All he could think about was the movie. He was *desperate* to see it. If Alex had been thinking clearly, he might have realized that this didn't make any sense. After all, he could watch *Night of the Living Dead* anytime he wanted to on his iPad—surely that was a better choice than knocking on strangers' doors in the middle of the night. Unfortunately, Alex was *not* thinking clearly. His green eyes, usually so sharp and inquisitive behind their glasses, had gone uncharacteristically flat, and his mouth hung open in a baffled expression, giving him a striking resemblance to one of the zombies from the movie.

Alex knocked on the door with three quick taps. A woman answered almost immediately, as though she had been expecting his arrival.

"Well, look at this," she said, peering down at him. "A visitor!"

The woman was in her late twenties, with dark skin and short, spiky hair. She wore all black and a lot of makeup, especially around the eyes.

"I'm sorry," Alex said, his mind swirling. *What am I doing here?* "I don't know why I knocked. I just heard . . ."

"What did you hear?" she asked, leaning forward with an eager expression. "Tell me."

"The movie."

The woman smiled. There were tiny gaps between her narrow teeth, giving her the look of one of those weird, glowing fish that prowl the deepest part of the ocean.

"A *movie*?" she asked, with genuine curiosity. "That's new. Which one?"

Alex gave the woman a strange look. He could still hear the television blaring behind her—the zombie now banging on the window of Barbara's car—yet she was acting like she heard nothing at all.

"Don't you know?" Alex asked.

"Why should I? The movie's for you, not me." She opened the door wider. "You want to watch it?" she asked. "I bet it's one of your favorites!"

A beam of fear cut through the fog of Alex's thoughts.

It's the middle of the night and I'm having a conversation with a total stranger like it's the most normal thing in the world, he thought. *What's wrong with me?*

He took a step back, intending to leave as quickly as possible . . . when he smelled something wonderful coming from the apartment.

Freshly baked pumpkin pie. His favorite.

He breathed in the comforting smells of nutmeg and cinnamon and all his fear instantly evaporated.

This woman isn't a threat, he thought. *She's just a nice lady who likes horror movies, like me!*

"The movie's *Night of the Living Dead,*" Alex said. "1968. Directed by George Romero."

"Ahh," said the woman. "How intriguing. And was I right? Is it one of your favorites?"

"Top ten. Right between *Let the Right One In* and *The Ring.*" Alex shrugged apologetically. "I like scary stuff."

"You sound like my kind of kid," the woman replied, grinning. "It's crazy—I was just about to kick back and watch the movie, when I thought, 'The only thing missing is someone to share this with, someone who really *appreciates* it,' and here you are!"

She opened the door all the way, allowing Alex a view of a comfortable-looking couch and a coffee table piled with oatmeal-raisin cookies and pumpkin pie. Across from this cozy setup, a huge TV played the black-and-white images he longed to see: Barbara staggering toward the farmhouse, where she would be trapped for the rest of the movie, with zombies in hot pursuit. Alex took a step forward, entranced.

"Well, don't just stand there gawking, silly boy," the woman said. "Come inside."

Even later, when Alex knew that he had been under the influence of a powerful spell, he found it hard to believe that he had entered the apartment so easily. At the time, it was like his body was not his own but a moth drawn to the flickering lights of the television.

He crossed the threshold. The door clicked shut behind him.

"Gotcha," the woman said under her breath.

She slipped a cold hand around his wrist and all the energy seemed to leave his body. Alex sank into the cushions of a nearby couch, barely able to keep his eyes open.

The woman eased into the chair across from him. The smile had faded from her lips.

"What's your name?" she asked.

"Alexander. Alex."

"Which one?"

"Alex," he said.

He looked around the apartment in confusion. The television had vanished, along with the coffee table and pumpkin pie.

"Where did the TV go?" Alex asked.

"It was never there."

"No," he insisted. "I *saw* it."

"The apartment does what it can to get you inside. Different for everyone. A movie is an odd choice. Traditionally, it's some sort of food that draws them. Kids are always thinking with their stomachs, you know."

"I smelled pumpkin pie."

"There you go."

It was becoming harder for Alex to focus. The room kept tilting back and forth, like when you first step off the pirate-ship ride at an amusement park. He felt like he might be ill.

"I want to go home," he said.

"Obviously that's not going to happen, Alex."

He turned in his seat, moving impossibly slow, hoping to make a mad dash for the door. Except the door had vanished. The place where it had once stood was nothing but a blank wall.

"Where did the door go?" he asked groggily.

"Away," the woman said. "Don't worry. You won't be needing it anymore."

"But that's not possible," Alex said. "Doors don't just . . . they can't . . ."

"Haven't you figured it out yet?" she asked, grinning with pride. "I'm a witch! Just like in a storybook." She touched a single fingernail to his forehead. "And you, little mouse, have fallen right into my trap."

Alex tried to stand, but his legs had turned to jelly and he collapsed to the floor instead. A wave of darkness crashed over him.

2

THE VOICE AT THE DOOR

Alex woke up in the lower half of a bunk bed. He had no idea where he was or how he had gotten there. He lay perfectly still, his body frozen with fear.

Gradually, the events of the previous night returned to him.

The elevator. The apartment.

The witch.

Except she's not really *a witch,* Alex thought, his mind racing. *Witches aren't real. She's just some crazy lady who* thinks *she's a witch. But then why did I see a TV that wasn't really there? Did she hypnotize me or something?*

Alex clutched his blanket as a question of more immediate concern popped into his head.

Who's sleeping on the top bunk?

He stared at the iron bars holding the mattress in place

above him, listening carefully for breathing sounds. When he didn't hear anything, Alex slid to the floor and gently placed his foot on the bottom rung of the ladder connecting the two bunks. In one swift movement, he popped his head over the upper railing. There was no one there, just an old mattress without any sheets or blanket. Alex let out a sigh of relief.

I never knew a bunk bed could be so scary, he thought.

The rest of the room was small and plainly furnished. There was a standing mirror in the corner and two doors. The first one Alex opened led to the closet, which was mostly empty except for some children's clothes hanging from the rod. Flipping through shirts, pants, and dresses of various sizes, Alex remembered something that the woman had said the previous night: *"Traditionally, it's some sort of food that draws them."*

Them, he thought, with a sickening feeling of dread. *I'm not the first.*

Of course, if he accepted what the woman had said at face value, that meant the apartment was capable of reading children's minds in order to lure them with the appropriate bait. *Like a smarter version of the candy house in "Hansel and Gretel,"* Alex thought. *In my case, a scary movie did the trick.* He stared at the clothes before him. *But what about these other kids? What brought them here? The smell of chocolate? A friend's voice?*

"No," Alex said. "That's impossible. There's no such thing as magic!"

He slammed the door shut with such ferocity that the empty hangers tinkled together in response. Even if he rejected magic as a factor, it still left the disturbing possibility that he was just one of a long line of children who had slept in this room. And, if he followed that train of thought to its final stop, Alex found himself facing an even more disturbing question: If he wasn't the first kid that she had taken, what had happened to the rest of them?

Before his overactive imagination could supply any morbid answers, Alex crossed the room to the second door, nearly tripping over his backpack in the process. This door was normal in every way except that it had two keyholes instead of one. The upper keyhole was the usual kind, but the second bore a strange crescent shape.

Probably a special lock, he thought, *to keep anyone from escaping.*

Alex was so certain that attempting to open the door would be a dead end that he gasped when the knob turned in his hand.

She must have forgotten to lock it, he thought with a faint glimmer of hope.

Sucking in his breath, Alex opened the door as slowly and quietly as he could. The next room looked identical to the first: simple bed, single closet, standing mirror in the corner. Alex stepped inside, wary of squeaking floorboards, and gently shut the door behind him.

The moment he did, the door vanished and became a regular wall.

"What?" Alex asked, backing away in shock until he tripped over something on the floor.

His backpack.

"It can't be," he said, shaking his head. "That's still in the other room!"

After he checked the contents, however, there could no longer be any doubt. Either his bag had somehow teleported from one room to another, or something even stranger was happening. Trembling slightly, he opened the closet door.

Children's clothes hung from the rod. They were identical in every way to the ones that he had been examining just a few minutes beforehand.

"It's the same room," Alex said in astonishment.

He opened the door with two keyholes and looked back and forth between the rooms, searching for the slightest difference. There wasn't any. He could even see the door open on the other side of the second room, and then an endless series of identical rooms beyond this, like reflections in a maze of mirrors. Curious what would happen, Alex lifted his backpack and watched its twin rise into the air like a prop in a haunted house.

It's a magical prison, he thought. *There's no way to escape.*

Alex shut the door and took a seat on the edge of the bed. The wheels of his brain spun madly, trying to process the giant wrecking ball that had just tilted his world askew.

Magic is real, he thought, his head in his hands.

He stayed like this for a long time, until he was struck by a second idea. Rising to his feet, Alex screamed as loud as he could while jumping up and down and pounding his fists against the wall, trying to make as much noise as possible.

"Help! I've been captured by a crazy woman! Call the police!"

This place may be magic, but it's still inside a New York City apartment building, he thought, *not some house in the middle of the woods. Someone will hear me! Someone will—*

The walls began to shake.

As a lifetime resident of the East Coast, Alex had never experienced an earthquake. What he was seeing and feeling right now, however—floor vibrating, walls shaking—was just as he had imagined an earthquake would be. Terror squeezed the air from his lungs. At any moment, Alex was certain that the floor would crack open and swallow him whole, or the ceiling would collapse, burying him beneath a mountain of rubble. . . .

And then it was over.

What was that? Alex thought. He fell to his knees and waited for his equilibrium to return. *That couldn't have been an earthquake, not in New York. But then what was it?*

Alex heard a scratching noise and saw the doorknob start to turn. He had just enough time to notice that a key had been inserted into the crescent keyhole, not the normal one, and then the witch entered the room.

"Why were you screaming?" she asked. "This apartment is enchanted. There could be an entire orchestra playing in the living room right now, and no one beyond these walls would hear a single note."

She was wearing a flowing black dress with black boots and black lipstick. Her long black nails came to ten sharp points. Around her neck hung a beetle encased in amber. It was black.

She sure looks *like a witch,* Alex thought. *All she's missing is a broom and a pointy hat.*

A dozen keys dangled from a ring in her hand. Some were the typical kind. Others were white and didn't look metallic at all.

"There was an earthquake or something," Alex said.

"That was just the apartment settling itself. It happens from time to time."

"Really?" Alex asked. "This felt pretty—"

The woman vanished before his eyes.

"Boo," she whispered in his ear, now standing behind him.

Alex screamed and stumbled backward, nearly losing his balance.

"That was amazing, wasn't it?" the woman asked, looking pleased with herself. "You want to see it again?"

Alex shook his head, unable to speak.

She's a witch, he thought. *A real, live, honest-to-goodness witch.*

"Please let me go," he finally managed, the words little more than a whisper. "I won't tell anyone about this, really."

"Alan, right?" she asked.

"Alex."

"Not Alexander," the woman said, remembering. "I'm Natacha. The thing of it is: I can't let you leave. Not now, not ever."

"Why not?" Alex asked. And then, in a voice that sounded impossibly small, he added, "Are you going to do something bad to me?"

"I'm a witch," she said. "You're a child. We're not going to play checkers. Ever read any fairy tales?"

Alex nodded.

"Then you know how it is." She sighed with exasperation. "I really don't have time for this today. I'm already late for an important meeting." Natacha looked him over, her eyes lingering on his stomach. She smirked. "You don't look like much of a worker. A few too many ice cream sundaes, perhaps? But then, what should I do with you?"

"You could let me go," Alex suggested.

"Oh," Natacha said. "You're funny. Unfortunately, that's not the same as being useful. Whatever. If things don't work out, I'll just add you to my collection." She brushed her hands together in a cleaning-up motion. "Problem solved."

"What does that—"

Natacha checked her watch and let out a high-pitched scream.

"Now you've made me even later than before! You've only been here a few hours and you're already a problem. Not a good sign, Alan!"

She slipped through the door and slammed it shut behind her. Alex heard the bolt click home.

Without any windows by which to judge the passing of time, the hours smudged together, making it difficult for Alex to determine how long he had been trapped inside the room. *Four hours?* he wondered. *Eight?* There was no use trying to escape. He had been back and forth between the two rooms at least a dozen times.

He didn't bother screaming anymore. Alex believed Natacha when she said that no one could hear him. After all, he had seen her vanish before his eyes and magically teleport across the room. Being able to soundproof her apartment didn't seem like much of a stretch.

Alex cried for a while. He tried not to, but he couldn't help it.

He felt cold and scared and alone—and a little disappointed. All his life he had loved scary stories, and now he was inside of one. It should have been fun. The problem was that the witches Alex had read about in books were *story* scary. This was *real* scary. It was a big difference.

What is she going to do to me when she gets home tonight? Alex wondered.

His imagination, as usual, leaped to the darkest conclusions. *She might eat me. Or boil me in a cauldron. Or chop me up into ingredients for a spell.* Gruesome images flashed through his mind, each worse than the last. Alex wanted to shut them off, but it wasn't as easy as turning a valve or flicking a switch. All he could do was wait it out.

Finally, he heard footsteps.

At first Alex thought that Natacha had returned, and his heart began to drum in his chest. *This is it,* he thought. Only instead of unlocking the door, the mysterious visitor hesitated just outside the room. A long shadow stretched beneath the crack of the door.

"Hello?" Alex asked. "Is somebody there?"

He heard faint breathing behind the door.

"Please!" he exclaimed. "She's going to be back soon! You have to help me!"

The silence stretched on and on. Alex was starting to wonder if his imagination was getting the best of him again when he heard a girl's soft voice.

"She likes stories."

Floorboards squeaked as the shadow beneath the door retreated. In moments, Alex was alone once again.

3

THE THING INSIDE THE BACKPACK

Alex knew he wasn't brave. He was terrified of roller coasters and pretty girls and losing his parents in a crowd. When older kids bumped into him in the hallway, intentionally or not, he always mumbled "my bad" and kept walking. Even math tests made him sweat.

Unfortunately, this was the type of situation where an unusual amount of bravery was required. Since Alex, by his own estimation, wasn't up to snuff, he tried to imagine what his big brother would do. It wasn't hard. John reacted to any sort of adversity with violence. They had a box full of broken video game controllers to prove it.

He would have knocked her out the first chance he got, Alex thought.

For the most part, Alex considered his older brother a walking meathead just a few IQ points north of a zombie, but a John-style approach seemed like his best bet. The moment that Natacha returned, he could shove her to the ground, grab her keys, dash out of the room, and lock the door behind him.

I'll have to surprise her before she has a chance to cast any spells, Alex thought. *That's the only way this will work.*

He pressed his foot against the leg of the bed in a sprinter's pose, his entire body angled toward the door. Every so often Alex stretched his muscles or cracked his neck, but other than that he remained still, imagining that he was a solider on sentry duty.

Finally, the doorknob turned.

Alex charged. Natacha entered the room, raised her eyebrows at the sight of his lumbering body, and waved her hand dismissively. Alex felt something clutch his ankles with an iron grip, and then his feet left the floor as he was yanked backward. After a painful landing, Alex looked behind him and saw the legs of the bed wrapped around his ankles like vines. As he watched, they withdrew and solidified into their previous shape.

Natacha stared down at Alex with a look of resignation, like he was an errand that could no longer be put off: a dirty floor, an empty refrigerator.

"My meeting went *great*!" she exclaimed, as though Alex had asked. "New customer. Placed a huge order, willing to pay double for it. Isn't that spectacular?"

Despite his predicament, Alex was curious. Story witches cursed newborns and spackled houses with sugary treats; they didn't run businesses.

"An order for what?" he asked.

"What do you think? Magic-infused oils, of course! Huge market for it. A hex for that annoying neighbor, extra luck for a weekend getaway to Atlantic City. And love oils." She rolled her eyes in disgust. "I am so sick of love oils. Then again, business is business."

Alex forced a smile. If he couldn't escape, he figured that he should at least stay on her good side.

"Congratulations," he said. "That's . . . really great."

"So sweet," she said, patting him on the head. "Unfortunately, since everything here is running so well, I don't want to throw any new cogs into the machine. If it ain't broke, don't fix it." She raised her hands into the air and they began to glow with blue light. "Just be a doll and stand still. And whatever you do, don't close your eyes. Like a photograph."

Natacha lowered her hands toward Alex's shoulders. He trembled with fear, knowing that there was nowhere to run, nothing he could do to stop her.

I just want to go home, Alex thought. *I just want to see my family again.*

Suddenly, he remembered what the girl had said. It was a long shot, but he had no other ideas.

"Do you want to hear a story?" he asked.

Natacha paused. Cocked her head to one side.

"What kind of story?" she asked.

"Scary."

Regarding Alex with skepticism, she flicked the blue light from her hands.

"Interesting," she said. "I wonder . . ." She shook her head. "Nah, you're just a boy! What kind of scary story can *you* know? Something you read in a library book? Heard around a campfire? I have no use for the same old tales."

"You couldn't have heard these," Alex said. "I made them up."

"That's even worse!" Natacha snapped. "I need *real* scary stories, not lame kiddie tales."

Alex flushed with anger.

"My stories *are* scary!" he exclaimed. "*Too* scary! That's why I was going to burn them all up last night!"

"That doesn't make any sense," she said. "If your stories are as good as you claim, why would you *destroy* them?"

Alex remained silent. His storytelling instincts told him that he should hold back on the details for now. Once Natacha knew everything, she wouldn't be interested anymore. And if he wanted to survive, he needed to keep her interested.

"Fine," she said. Natacha clapped her hands together

and a shadowy chair rose from the floor. She eased into it and stared at him expectantly. "Tell us a story. Let's see what you've got."

Alex picked up his backpack with sweaty palms.

"What are you doing?" Natacha asked.

"My nightbooks are inside," he said.

"Nightbooks?"

"The journals I write my stories in," he said. "I have trouble sleeping. Bad dreams. The only way to get rid of them is to write them down."

"Nightbooks," Natacha said. She smacked her lips together as though tasting the word. "I like that."

Bending down on one knee, Alex unzipped the front of the backpack and withdrew a marbled composition book with his name printed neatly on the front. *Which story should I read?* he thought. There were dozens of possibilities in this nightbook alone. Alex knew that if he picked a bad one he wouldn't get a second chance.

"Something short," Natacha said, growing impatient. "An appetizer to see if I want to stay for the entire meal."

Alex spread the nightbook open, flipping through the pages with shaking hands. Finally, he settled on something that he thought might work.

If she doesn't like this, I'm a goner, he thought.

He started to read.

LOST DOG

The first time that Greg saw the dog was at his friend Eric's house. The two boys had been hanging out all day, and after finally getting bored of video games they went outside to throw the Frisbee around. The dog was sitting on the front porch. It was a medium-sized animal with mangy white fur, like an old undershirt that had been worn one time too many. Neither boy recognized the breed.

"Hey there," said Eric, bending down to scratch the dog's neck.

The dog didn't wag its tail. It stared up at Eric with sad eyes.

"Must be lost," Greg said, keeping his distance. (His mother, who had been bitten when she was a girl, had always warned him to stay away from strange animals.) "Check the tag. Maybe he belongs to one of your neighbors."

Eric inspected the tag on the chain collar. It was a shiny black triangle without any name or address.

"Weird," said Eric, pinching the strange tag between his fingers. "Feel this. It's as cold as ice."

"I'm good," Greg said, backing away. The dog was looking at him with those sad eyes. Greg couldn't say why, but he suddenly wanted to get out of there as quickly as possible. "I'm heading home."

The next morning, his parents sat him down at the dining room table and gave him the tragic news: There had been an electrical fire while Eric and his family were sleeping. None of them had survived.

A year passed. Greg was still sad when he thought about Eric, but not as sad as he used to be. One day he was walking home from school when he passed the Wilsons' house. The lawn hadn't been mowed in a while and mail was overflowing from the mailbox. No one held these things against them. Their daughter, Rennae, was sick. Not stay-home-from-school sick, but the bad kind that required overnight stays at the hospital.

A white dog stared out at him from the Wilsons' front window.

Until that point, Greg had forgotten all about the lost dog that he had seen at Eric's house the day of the fire. Now the memory came rushing back. *It can't be the same one*, he thought. *Can it?* He crossed the lawn to get a closer look. The dog sat as still as a statue and stared back at him with sad eyes.

A black triangle dangled from its collar.

Greg ran home. The next morning, his mom got a phone call that made her break down into tears.

Rennae Wilson had died in her sleep.

After that, Greg started looking for the white dog everywhere he went. He never saw it. Eventually he became convinced that the dog had just been a figment of his imagination.

One beautiful summer day, Greg went to an amusement

park. They had just built a new roller coaster. It was one of the tallest in the world, and Greg had been waiting all year to ride it. At first his mom said no—there had been stories online about some safety concerns—but Greg finally talked her into it. He waited for hours to get the front seat. As he pulled the shoulder harness over his chest, he knew that it had been worth it.

The car climbed the hill ever so slowly, higher and higher and higher. Greg looked down and gasped at how small the people had gotten below him. He grinned.

This is going to be great, he thought.

There were tiny steps along the side of the track, just in case a worker needed to get up there and fix something. At the very top of the hill was a small platform just big enough for someone to stand on. The white dog was there, watching the coaster ascend. Its eyes looked sadder than ever. Sunlight glinted off its triangular collar.

Greg knew that the dog's presence could mean only one thing.

"Stop the ride!" he shouted, struggling against his shoulder harness.

It was too late. The roller coaster was already plunging down the first drop. All around Greg, people started to scream.

Alex closed the nightbook. Natacha stared at him for a long time, eyes narrowed.

She hated it, he thought. *I've blown my only chance.*

"You really wrote that?" she finally asked.

Alex nodded.

"You sure?" Natacha asked. "Maybe you read a story that you liked in a book and you copied it down, told everyone that you were the real writer. . . ."

"I would never do that!" Alex insisted—his anger, for now, overriding his fear. "It's *my* story. I can even tell you where I got the idea. My friend found this dog one day and I got to wondering, What if the Grim Reaper had a pet?"

Natacha raised her eyebrows in amusement.

"Most kids would have just thrown the dog a ball and called it a day," she said.

"That's other kids," Alex said, twisting the nightbook in his hands. "They play with dogs. I play with *what ifs*. I wish I could be more like them, but it's not something I can control."

"No," Natacha said with a knowing smile. "I imagine not."

She continued to stare at him, absentmindedly tweezing a strand of shadows from the arm of the magic chair and spooling it around her index finger.

"Did you . . . like it?" Alex finally asked, hating the uncertainty in his voice, his need to know. He rarely shared his writing, but when he did his hunger for immediate feedback bordered on desperate.

"Wrong question," Natacha said.

She rose from the shadow chair—which dissipated into the air—and pressed her ear against the nearest wall like a safe cracker.

"What are you doing?" Alex asked.

"Shh."

Natacha listened closely. Finally, she nodded with satisfaction.

"Good," she said. "Yes, that will do."

"What will do?" Alex asked. "What are you talking about?"

The witch ignored him and opened the door leading out of the room. Alex caught a glimpse of an ordinary-looking hallway.

"Sleep well, storyteller," Natacha said, just before leaving the apartment. "Tomorrow your real work begins."

She locked the door behind her.

4

A ROOM OF DARK WONDERS

Alex was awoken by the sounds of his mom and dad in the kitchen as they made a big breakfast together, just like they did every Saturday: voices, laughter, the clatter of pots and pans. The moment he opened his eyes, however, the noises vanished. It had only been a cruel bridge between dreaming and waking.

I'm not home, Alex remembered, orienting himself. *I was kidnapped by a witch.*

He closed his eyes, not yet ready to abandon the relative safety of his bed, and thought about his family. *Who discovered I was missing?* Not his brother, John; he had to catch the early bus on Friday. Not his dad, either. He was never the first to rise, clinging to those final moments of sleep like a life raft.

It must have been Mom.

Alex pictured her walking into his room and seeing his empty bed. She wouldn't panic, not at first. She would just assume that he was already up, probably eating breakfast or using the bathroom. Soon, however, she would notice that Alex's bag was gone, at which point she would call the school to see if he had taken the early bus for some reason.

When they tell her I'm not there, Alex thought, *that's when it'll hit her. That's when she'll wake up Dad.*

Alex wondered if they had called the police yet. He imagined his parents holding hands on their couch, talking to a man in a blue uniform dutifully taking notes on a small pad, and felt such pure love for them that he had to fight back tears.

This is all my fault, he thought. *If I hadn't snuck out in the middle of the night to get rid of my nightbooks, none of this would have happened. Then again, if I wasn't such a stupid freak who wrote stupid freaky stories in the first place—*

Alex opened his eyes.

Thinking about the past wasn't going to help. Right now the most important thing was to remain calm and figure out a way to escape. The greatest apology he could give his parents was to return home safe and sound.

Thus resolved, Alex sat up . . . and promptly banged his head. *Bunk bed!* he thought, clasping a hand to his forehead. *I forgot!*

The mattress above him squeaked as something shifted its weight.

"Hello?" Alex asked, frozen. "Someone there?"

No answer.

Heart hammering in his chest, Alex backed across the floor until he reached a vantage point that allowed him to see the upper bunk. There was a massive orange lump lying on the mattress. Green eyes watched his every move.

What is it? Alex wondered. *Some kind of monster?*

He grabbed a lamp and raised it over his head, just in case the creature decided to slither down the ladder and attack. While he waited, Alex took a closer look.

He burst into laughter.

"You're just a cat!" he exclaimed.

It was, in fact, the fattest cat that he had ever seen. Its fur was pumpkin orange with just the slightest hint of dark stripes. Black fur encircled, and accentuated, its piercing green eyes. The cat's most unusual feature, however, was a long tail that arced straight into the air before spiraling into a neat question mark.

"You look like a cat that ate a raccoon," Alex said. "Or a monkey. Or both."

The cat, who hadn't moved from its spot on the top bunk, seemed unamused by this assessment. It gazed down at Alex like a queen from her throne.

"I didn't realize Natacha had a pet," Alex said, putting

the lamp back and climbing halfway up the ladder. He reached up and stroked the cat beneath its chin. It did not purr, or show any sign of pleasure whatsoever, but rather bore his touch like some kind of foul-tasting medicine best swallowed as quickly as possible.

"You're not the friendliest thing, are you?" Alex asked. "That's okay. Glad to have any company at all." He scanned the room, curious how the cat had managed to slip inside, and received his second surprise of the morning: the door with the two keyholes was open wide. Instead of providing passage into an identical room, as before, the doorway now opened into a long hallway.

"This is crazy," Alex said, repositioning his glasses on his nose as though that might change what he was seeing. "What happened to the other room?"

He directed this question toward the cat. It wasn't that he expected an answer; it was just comforting to talk to another living thing. The cat, however, did not seem eager for companionship. It looked back at him with a condescending expression: *Stop talking to me. I'm a cat.*

"Okay," Alex said, feeling a giddy rumbling in his stomach that was equal parts nervousness, excitement, and good old-fashioned hunger. "Time to explore."

He walked down a dimly lit hallway, passing a single door to either side of him. They each had two keyholes: regular and crescent-shaped. *They're probably bedrooms,*

Alex thought, thinking about the layout of his own apartment. *Maybe one of them belongs to the girl whose voice I heard.* He considered knocking, but didn't want to risk waking Natacha. Instead, he stood perfectly still and listened carefully, hearing nothing. After a brief moment of hesitation, he tried turning the knobs.

Locked.

At the end of the hallway was a small bathroom. There was no crescent keyhole on this door, and Alex was relieved to find it unlocked.

He entered the living room.

The furniture was expensive old, the red wallpaper patterned with black flowers. If Alex had not already met the apartment's owner, he would have assumed that she was far older than Natacha, for this was a grandmotherly type of room. Not the nice sort of grandma who pinched your cheeks and baked chocolate chip cookies, but the creepy kind who rocked back and forth while knitting sweaters for dead children. Fancy display cases lined the walls, their shelves filled with mysterious objects that looked like they were on loan from some museum of dark magic. Alex saw wands resting upon silver pedestals, black jars with intriguing labels such as "Last Breaths" and "Vampiric Ashes," horrific masks that seemed to watch him as he passed, tomes whose spines had been embossed with unrecognizable symbols, and an entire display case packed with crystal balls.

"Cool," Alex said.

Most children would have been frightened by such witchy paraphernalia, but Alex, who constructed his own Halloween advent calendar every October first, was fascinated. *What does this thing do?* he wondered, bending down to look more closely at a mummified hand. He supposed that he should have been more frightened than ever, since Natacha's impressive collection suggested that she was a powerful witch indeed, and yet Alex couldn't keep the grin off his face.

Creepy things were *awesome.*

On a nearby shelf, he saw a fancy black chest about the size of a shoe box. Until this point, he had resisted the urge to touch anything; just because he thought the objects were wonderful did not mean he was ignorant of their potential dangers. At the very least, they looked valuable. Natacha would probably turn him into a frog or something if she caught him touching one.

Still, his curiosity gnawed at him.

What's in the chest? Maybe something amazing . . . the most amazing thing of all. . . .

"Hello?" Alex called out, testing the silence. "Natacha? Anybody home?"

No one answered. Even the cat was nowhere to be seen.

"Okay," he said, stretching his hand toward the chest. "I'm just going to take a quick peek. . . ."

Something hissed behind him.

Alex froze in place, and then—slowly—looked over his shoulder. The orange cat was glaring up at him. It had appeared seemingly out of nowhere.

"Where did you—" Alex started, and then swallowed the rest of his sentence as he took in the cat's menacing pose. It had looked harmless enough just a few minutes ago, but not anymore. Its back was arched, its fangs bared: a return to predatory roots.

Alex, uncertain what had caused this change in the cat's attitude, was afraid to move, afraid to even breathe.

Then he noticed that the cat's eyes were not on him at all. They were on the black chest—or, perhaps, his fingers, just inches from it. He slowly withdrew his hand. The cat relaxed, its face returning to its default expression of bored superiority.

"Is it because I was going to touch the chest?" Alex asked. "Is it off-limits?"

He found it hard to believe that a cat could be that intelligent. Of course, up until very recently, he believed that magic and witches could only be found in stories. There was clearly a lot he didn't know.

No big deal, he thought, leaving the chest alone for now and reaching instead for a straw doll a few shelves away.

There's plenty of other interesting stuff here.

The cat hissed even louder than before.

Alex snapped his hand back. The cat instantly relaxed.

"You're like my own personal guard," Alex said, putting it together. "That's your job, isn't it? To make sure I don't touch anything I'm not supposed to touch?"

The cat puffed out its chest, acknowledging Alex's theory.

"Got it," he said, raising his hands into the air. "Look. No touching."

In a way, he was grateful for the cat's intervention. The magical objects had been a distraction; he needed to look for a way out of the apartment. Alex decided to start with the most logical point: the front door . . . or, at least, the place where the front door *should* have been. Right now it was just a wall.

Must be a spell, he thought. *Natacha can come and go through the front door whenever she wants, but no one else can leave the apartment.*

Wondering if he'd be able to hear any residents in the outside hallway, Alex pressed his ear against the wall. There were no voices, but beneath the wall's paper skin he heard a rushing sound punctuated by rhythmic grinding. It was muffled and faint.

Maybe it's the sound of the elevator gears grinding together, Alex thought.

He remembered how Natacha had listened to the

bedroom wall after he read his story last night. *Was that the sound that she heard?* he wondered. *If so, why did she seem so pleased?*

He had no idea.

In any case, the front door was a dead end for now, so Alex decided to check the nearest window. He expected to see downtown Flushing: signs in Korean and Chinese, parked cars squeezed tightly together, piles of black garbage bags awaiting pickup.

Instead, he saw a mirror image of the room he was standing in.

"It's the same magic as the bedroom door," Alex said. "If I climb through the window, I'll just end up back where I started from."

How can I escape from a place that has no exits?

Feeling somewhat dispirited, he explored the rest of the apartment, the cat his second shadow. The floor plan was identical to his own home, so he knew exactly what to expect: a dining area barely large enough to fit table and chairs, a washer and dryer unit tucked into an alcove, and three additional closets (pantry, linens, coats). In the small kitchen two peanut butter sandwiches and a glass of milk waited on the counter. Alex had no idea if they were meant for him or not, but he hadn't eaten for nearly two days and gobbled them down.

Compared to the living room, the rest of the apartment

was surprisingly ordinary. Two of the closets had crescent-shaped keyholes in addition to the ordinary ones, but other than that Alex didn't come across anything else with a magical vibe. There was one thing that gave him the creeps, however. In the dining room, an antique china cabinet displayed a collection of brightly painted figurines. They were all children engaged in some manner of play. A girl skipping rope. A boy catching a butterfly with a net. A dozen more: tossing a ball, splashing in a pond, reading on a park bench.

Alex was staring at the painfully wide smile of a little girl riding a sled when he heard a scratching noise to his left. He spun around and looked through the archway that separated the dining and living rooms.

Someone was unlocking the coat closet from the inside.

Impossible! Alex thought. *I just checked that closet like five minutes ago. There was no one there! It wasn't even locked!*

The key scratched again. It wasn't a metallic sound, like a normal key would make—more like chalk clicking against a blackboard. It seemed to be coming from the crescent-shaped keyhole.

It's Natacha, Alex thought, preparing himself. *Does she know I've been snooping around her apartment? Is she going to punish me?*

The door swung open.

5

THE OTHER PRISONER

The girl who stepped into the living room looked as though she had risen from the grave. Dirt matted her hands and face. Stains splattered her brown apron. Dark goggles concealed her eyes.

Alex, whose nerves were already at their breaking point, did what anyone else would have done in that situation.

He screamed.

"What?" the girl asked, looking behind her for the cause of Alex's terror, as though something far more horrible had followed her through the closet door. "What is it?"

She removed her goggles. Instead of the red, demonic orbs that Alex had been expecting, her eyes were big and brown and staring at him with undisguised annoyance.

Alex suddenly felt very foolish.

"Sorry," he said. "I thought you might have been . . . you know."

"I really don't."

"A zombie or something."

The girl mulled this over.

"Good news," she said. "I'm alive. And a vegetarian. I think you're in the clear."

The girl sighed with annoyance and brushed past him. Alex followed her into the kitchen, where she filled a glass with water at the sink and downed the entire thing.

"I was supposed to show you around this morning," she finally said, in the bitter tone of a teacher who hated her job. "That's why Natacha unlocked your door. But you were in a majorly deep slumber and I didn't feel like dealing with a grumpy new kid, so I let you sleep." The girl glared at him angrily, as though all of this had been Alex's fault. "Had to start without you. Last thing I need is for Natacha to come home and see I haven't gotten all my chores done. You snore, by the way."

"I know."

"I could hear you through the door. Pretty impressive. That's not just any door, as you've probably noticed. That's a *magic*—"

"Who are you?" Alex asked, with more bite than he intended. The girl's attitude was starting to grate on his nerves.

"My name's Yasmin," she said. "Not Jasmine. No *j*, no *e*. People always screw it up. Drives me crazy."

"I'm Alex."

"I know. I went through your bag while you were snoring away, saw your name on those notebooks."

Alex reddened. Despite everything that had happened, he still didn't want anyone to read his nightbooks.

"You read my stories?" he asked.

"Chill," Yasmin said, raising her hands in a pacifying gesture. "I didn't read them. I tried to, but I gave up. You have the worst handwriting I've ever seen. Like, seriously, you're the reason typing was invented. But the books made me think of Scheherazade, from all those stories my *sito* used to tell me."

"Who's Schehara . . . Scheheri . . . ?"

"Scheherazade," Yasmin said. "From *The Arabian Nights*. She's the vizier's daughter, and she ends up getting imprisoned by this king with a habit of beheading his wives. In order to stay alive, she tells him a different story each night and stops in the middle, so he has to keep her around to find out how it ends." She sighed at his look of incomprehension. "You must have at least heard of the stories! 'Sinbad the Sailor,' 'Aladdin,' 'Ali Baba and the—'"

"You're the one who came to my door yesterday, aren't you?" Alex asked, finally making the connection. "You told me that Natacha liked stories. That's probably the only reason I'm still alive. You saved my life."

Alex thought Yasmin would be happy to hear these words, but instead she flinched as though he had insulted her. Her expression, which had grown almost friendly while she talked about *The Arabian Nights*, hardened into its previous look of disdain.

"I didn't save anything," she snapped. "You're still trapped here, just like me."

"So you're a prisoner, too?"

Yasmin pulled a battered Mets hat from her back pocket and jammed it on her head.

"Nah," she said. "I'm here on vacation."

"I thought that since you had your own key to the closet you might be, I don't know . . ."

. . . *the witch's apprentice,* he was about to add, but then he considered the girl's gaunt frame and haunted eyes. *She's being kept here against her will,* he thought, *just like me.*

"How long have you been here?" he asked softly.

"Long enough," she said, picking up the empty plate on the counter. "I see you found the sandwiches I made."

"Thank you," Alex said. "I was starving."

"Good thing you like peanut butter," Yasmin said. "I used to, too. There's a giant jar of it underneath the kitchen sink. Some crackers and instant oatmeal, too. Help yourself, but don't overdo it. Natacha isn't great about remembering to restock—our supplies, at least." Yasmin opened the refrigerator door, revealing shelves that were jam-packed with expensive food. "This—along with anything in the other cabinets—is off-limits. And don't think, 'She'll never know if I eat this one little chocolate.' She'll always know. Lenore tells her everything."

"Lenore?"

"Where is she, anyway?" Yasmin asked, looking around. "Lenore! Stop messing around."

The orange cat suddenly appeared at Alex's feet, startling him.

"It can turn itself invisible?" Alex asked in disbelief.

"It's a she," said Yasmin. "And yes—she can vanish at will. Lenore gives Natacha a full report on our activities each day. Just assume she's in the room with you at all times. Even when you don't think she's watching, trust me . . . she's watching."

Alex bent down and held his hand out, palm up, waiting for Lenore to approach him. She refused to acknowledge his presence.

"What are you doing?" Yasmin asked.

"Trying to make friends."

"Lenore doesn't want to be your friend," she said. "She's a witch's familiar. You know what that is?"

"A magical servant," Alex said. "I wrote a story once

about a familiar that tried to steal its master's spell book. Well, tried to write it. Couldn't figure out a good ending." He bent down again, trying to meet the cat's eyes. "I like your name. Lenore. Like in 'The Raven.'" He looked up at Yasmin. "Natacha must be an Edgar Allan Poe fan."

"He write creepy stories?"

"Oh yeah."

"Then I'm sure she is," Yasmin said. "Listen, this is fun and all, the bonding, but I have to get you set up so I can get back to real work."

"Set up doing what?"

Yasmin rolled her eyes, like an older sister saddled with babysitting duty.

"Just follow me."

She crossed past him back into the living room. Alex had to rush to keep up. Yasmin's walk was practically a run.

"The rules are pretty simple," she said, not even looking over her shoulder to see if he was following her. "Don't touch anything, especially the magical-looking stuff. Don't try to escape. It won't do any good, and if Natacha finds out . . ." She shook her head. "It's not worth the risk."

"Where is Natacha?" Alex asked.

Yasmin shrugged. "Out and about, I guess, selling her oils. She usually comes back around dinner. I cook, by the way. You clean."

Yasmin stopped at the door to the linen closet and withdrew a small ring with three white keys. *Like the ones Natacha had,* Alex thought, getting a good look at them for the first time. They were far more complicated than normal keys. Each bit had been carved into an intricate pattern of notches and swirls.

Alex reached over to touch the key pinched between Yasmin's fingers. It was cool and perfectly smooth.

"Are these carved from *bone*?" he asked.

"Yeah," Yasmin said, yanking the key away. "And don't ask me where the bones came from. I don't know, and I don't want to know."

She slipped the key into the crescent-shaped keyhole. It refused to turn.

"Stuck again," she muttered, shaking her head in frustration. It was clear that she wanted to get rid of Alex as quickly as possible, and this was just another roadblock.

"Why do some doors have two keyholes?" Alex asked.

"Well, Natacha can hardly keep the magical rooms out in the open," Yasmin said, jiggling the key back and forth, "just in case the super or someone comes poking around. So she hides them. The regular keys lead to regular places. The bonekeys, on the other hand . . ."

The key turned with a satisfying click. Yasmin pushed the door open.

Alex gasped.

He should have been looking at a tiny closet barely deep enough to hold an assortment of sheets, towels, and blankets. Instead, he stepped into a circular chamber that resembled the interior of a lighthouse. A narrow wooden staircase wound upward in tight spirals past hundreds of book-lined shelves, the ceiling a barely visible dot in the distance.

"This . . . *can't*," Alex said.

The room spun. Alex bent over and trained his eyes on the floor. The floor was real. The floor made sense.

"It's some sort of trick," he murmured.

"No trick," Yasmin said. "Just magic." When Alex didn't reply, she spoke again with a hint of sympathy. "Give it a minute. It's hard to get your mind around it at first, the idea that a room can be bigger than it ought to be. You're used to walls and ceilings meaning something."

Alex grappled with this wild idea, trying to hold it still. For a reason not immediately clear to him, he flashed back to something he had learned in Language Arts last year. "Good stories," Ms. Coral had said, "build their own worlds. Events that might seem crazy or unlikely in reality can make perfect sense within the right context. That's called interior logic."

Alex remembered the feeling of excitement bubbling within him as he giddily copied the words in his notebook. *INTERIOR LOGIC!!!* It was like being given permission to imagine anything he wanted, as long as he built the right fence to contain it.

Same thing here, he thought, finding a way that he could make sense of all this without losing his mind. *Magic rooms are impossible in the real world. But inside a witch's apartment that lures its victims with classic horror movies? Not so crazy.*

"Interior logic," he whispered.

Alex cautiously looked up again. The room was no longer spinning, but the floor still felt as if it was rocking beneath his feet. Taking deep breaths, Alex tried to anchor himself by picking out specific details that proved he was standing in a real place. Book spines of all shapes, sizes, and colors. Dust motes falling like snow. The musty smell of pages begging to be turned.

Finally, the room settled into place. His disorientation changed to excitement.

It's a library!

Grinning now, Alex walked over to the nearest shelf and read some of the titles: *The Empty Classroom and Other Creepy Stories, Nightdreams and Daymares, Tales to Whisper in Little Ears.*

"They're story collections," Alex said.

"*Scary* stories," Yasmin said. "Every book here."

Alex whistled, craning his neck to take in the rows of books spiraling over his head. *How many are there?* he wondered. *Five thousand? Ten thousand?*

"Natacha really does like stories," Alex said. "You weren't kidding."

"She makes me pick out a new book every night and read her a bedtime story," Yasmin said with clear distaste. "Some of them are good, some not so much. Either way, Natacha always seems disappointed. I think she's read all these books already, maybe more than once. She's dying for something new." Yasmin gave him a crooked smile. "And—ta-da!—here you come, the answer to her prayers. Her own personal story machine."

She nodded toward a simple wooden desk in the middle of the floor. It was empty except for a jar of pencils and a fresh pile of lined paper.

"This is where you'll be working," Yasmin said. "Every day, from morning to night, writing as many stories as possible."

Lenore suddenly appeared on a stool in the corner, giving her a perfect vantage point of the desk. The meaning in her cold green eyes was clear: *And I'll be watching you to make sure you do what Natacha wants.*

"This is crazy," Alex said.

"Totally," Yasmin said, "but do it anyway. Natacha's serious about this, Alex. You don't want to cross her. Besides, sitting in a nice comfy chair all day, making up stories—it could be worse."

Alex looked at Yasmin's dirt-encrusted nails, the long scratches on her arms.

"What does Natacha make you do?" he asked.

Yasmin started to say something, then glanced over at Lenore, as though unsure how much she should share.

"That doesn't concern you," Yasmin said.

She turned, meaning to leave, but Alex blocked her path. He lowered his voice to a soft whisper so Lenore couldn't hear him.

"There has to be a way out," he said. "If we work together—"

Yasmin pushed him away.

"Have I given you the impression that we're friends?" she asked. "Because we're not." She eyed Lenore, who was watching the conversation carefully. "And we're *definitely* not going to try and escape!"

"But—"

Yasmin jabbed her finger into his chest.

"No *but*. No nothing. This is your life now. Forget your family. Forget your friends. Focus on making yourself useful to Natacha." She met his eyes, warning him. "Write your stories, Alex. Entertain her. That's the only way you'll survive."

Alex didn't love this idea. After all, his nightbooks were what had caused all this trouble in the first place. But right now he didn't have any other plan.

"How long did telling stories work for Scheherazade?" Alex asked.

"One thousand and one nights," Yasmin replied.

"That's a long time," he said. "I think I'd go crazy before then."

Yasmin gave him a grim look.

"Don't worry," she said. "I doubt you'll last that long."

6

THE MISTING ROOM

Alex sat at the desk a long time, staring at a blank piece of paper. He figured it was safest to follow Natacha's instructions for now, but unfortunately he couldn't think of anything to write. It didn't help that he could feel Lenore's eyes on him, watching his every move. He was used to writing in the middle of the night without a single sound to disturb him.

"Could you go somewhere else?" Alex finally asked, glaring at the cat. "I can't concentrate with you staring at me like that."

Lenore vanished.

"That doesn't help!" Alex exclaimed. "I know you're still there!"

After a few moments, the cat reappeared on top of the desk. Alex nearly fell backward in surprise. Lenore sauntered back to her spot on the stool.

"This is why people like dogs," Alex muttered.

He pulled out a pencil and started writing random sentences on the paper, just to look like he was working. To be honest, Lenore wasn't the only reason he couldn't concentrate. Unanswered questions pulled his mind in all directions:

Can I trust Yasmin? Is there a way out of this apartment? What's that sound behind the walls, and why was Natacha so interested in it?

Am I ever going to see my family again?

Then there were the books.

Like all writers, Alex was, first and foremost, a reader, and it was impossible to focus on his own story when so many other ones lay within easy reach. His gaze strayed to the tantalizing volumes winding along the spiral staircase, a thousand worlds begging to be explored.

I'll pick a book at random and read a single story, Alex finally decided. *Just to get it out of my system.*

The moment he approached the staircase, however, Lenore leaped off her stool and blocked his path. She didn't hiss, but there was no mistaking the threat in her eyes.

Stop wasting time, she seemed to say. *Do your work.*

Alex thought about testing her—she was just a cat, after all—but then he remembered the long scratches on Yasmin's arms and decided to return to his seat. *No sense being reckless,* he thought, *not until I have a better idea what's going on here.* He was starting to get hungry again, but he figured he should at least get a few words down before eating, just in case Natacha came home and checked his progress. He pulled out a fresh sheet of paper and hunched over it, pencil in hand. *What should I write about?* he thought. *Monsters? Ghosts? School?*

As hard as he tried, the ideas refused to come. After another fruitless hour the grumbling in his stomach proved impossible to ignore. Alex rose from his seat.

Lenore looked up, annoyed by the disturbance.

"I'm just getting something to eat," Alex said. "That okay with you?"

The cat stretched languorously in response, then dropped to the floor with surprising grace and waited for Alex to lead the way. He passed through the closet door (feeling a sense of relief upon returning to the apartment, like that first footstep on solid ground after a long boat ride) and entered the kitchen. As Yasmin had promised, there wasn't much of a selection in the cabinet beneath the kitchen sink, just bread, stale crackers, a few cans of tuna fish, and a jar of store-brand peanut butter. After digging behind some cleaning supplies, however, Alex discovered a half-filled box of Froot Loops only slightly past its expiration date.

"Look at this!" he exclaimed, showing the box to the uninterested cat. "My favorite! If it was Cap'n Crunch or

Grape Nuts, I might have given up all hope, but this makes me think that everything might end up okay!" He popped a handful of Froot Loops into his mouth; they were stale but delicious. "You want some?"

Alex placed a few Froot Loops in his open palm and held his hand out to Lenore. She sniffed the multicolored rings cautiously.

"Go ahead," he said. "You'll like them. Everyone does."

Lenore bent forward, opening her mouth the slightest bit. Then she backed away, fixing Alex with a look of distrust.

"Your loss," Alex said, returning the Froot Loops to their hiding spot like buried treasure.

He returned to his bedroom and pulled a nightbook from his backpack. "I'm not going to finish a new story by tonight," he told Lenore, "so I might as well pick one that I've already written. That okay with you?" Lenore didn't seem thrilled by this change of plans, but she didn't do anything to stop him, either. As Alex settled into the antique love seat in the living room, she vanished as a mild form of protest.

He held the nightbook in front of his face and pretended to search for a story. His true attention, however, was focused just above the book, on the wall directly across from him.

It was the place where the front door should have been.

Alex hadn't exactly lied to Lenore; he really did want to pick out a good story. In fact, there was a part of him that was even looking forward to sharing his writing with Natacha tonight. But that wasn't the main purpose of his plan. Mostly, he wanted to see what happened when Natacha reentered the apartment. Despite Yasmin's warning, Alex was still set on escaping, and he needed a better understanding of how the only exit from the apartment worked.

He watched. He waited.

Finally, Natacha came home.

The transformation was simple: one moment there was a wall and the next moment there was a door. Natacha opened it and stepped across the threshold. Her hair and clothes were soaking wet. Alex heard no rain or thunder through the windows of the apartment, but it must have been pouring outside.

"Girl!" Natacha screamed. "Girl—get me some towels, now!" She shook her head and water flew everywhere. "Knew I should have brought an umbrella, but I hate lugging those things everywhere I go."

She sat down and tried to pull off a single boot. It made a big sucking sound, like a shoe embedded in mud, but refused to budge.

"Girl!" she screamed, her face growing red. "Where are you?"

Alex realized two things at the same time.

One, Natacha hadn't noticed that he was sitting there.

Two, she had left the front door wide open.

Alex heard his brother's voice in his head—*Move, freakazoid!*—and barreled toward freedom. He caught a glimpse of Natacha digging one finger into her ear, looking remarkably unconcerned by his escape attempt, and then he leaped forward . . .

. . . and slammed straight into a wall where the door had been.

Natacha, now digging in her other ear, gave Alex a dismissive glance as he slid to the ground.

"Girl!" she screamed. "Where are those towels?"

Dinner—for Natacha, at least—was chicken medallions sautéed in garlic sauce, corn on the cob, and mounds of mashed potatoes with gravy. Alex's stomach grumbled watching her eat it all, but he didn't say a word, just stood in the corner and occasionally refilled her glass with fresh lemonade when beckoned. After his failed attempt to pass through the front door, Alex figured that he should take a wait-and-see approach before hatching any new escape plans.

While Natacha ate dessert—a homemade brownie topped with vanilla ice cream and hot fudge—Alex cleared the table and washed the dishes. By the time he entered the living room, Natacha was waiting for him. She sat in a huge chair of luxurious black leather, its wooden frame spiraling upward into three tall spires. Alex thought it looked like the chair of an evil queen too poor to afford a proper throne.

"It's about time," Natacha said. She gestured toward a far humbler chair to her right. "Sit."

Alex lowered himself onto the chair. Yasmin was sitting on the antique love seat directly across from him. She looked meekly down at her lap. In Natacha's presence, she was a completely different girl from the one he had met earlier.

Alex picked up the nightbook he had left on the side table and prepared to read.

"Wait!" Natacha snapped. "Do I look ready to you? I haven't even set up my misting room yet!"

"I don't know what that is."

"And whose fault is *that*?"

Alex bit back a snarky response. *No good can come of making her mad,* he thought. Instead, he waited patiently while Natacha traced her finger through the air like someone scanning book spines for a specific title. *What the heck is she doing?* he wondered. After searching a bit longer, Natacha squeezed her thumb and index finger together and drew her hand down as though unzipping the very air itself. There was a tiny hissing noise like a leaking tire, and Natacha reached into what seemed to be an invisible pocket, her arm vanishing up to the elbow.

She noticed Alex's astonished expression and grinned with pleasure.

"This is some kind of spell, ain't it?" she asked. "You know any other witch that can do magic like this?"

"I don't know any other witches."

"Well, they *can't*!" Natacha screeched, digging deeper into the invisible hole. "You should consider yourself very lucky."

She withdrew her arm. There was a red cylinder in her hand. It had a tiny hole at the top and two buttons on the side.

"What's that?" Alex asked.

"An oil diffuser," Natacha said, setting it on the stand next to her.

"Oh," Alex said, disappointed. He wondered why Natacha would bother to hide such a common machine. "My mom has one of those. She uses it to make our living room smell nice when we have visitors."

"This one's a little different," Natacha said.

She reached into her pocket and produced a glass vial filled with blue liquid that swirled like a miniature storm.

"What's that?" Alex asked.

"Hey, storyteller," Natacha said. She poured the vial into the hole at the top of the diffuser. "Do you know what happens to children who ask too many questions?"

Alex shook his head.

“Me either,” Natacha said. “Because no one ever hears from them again!”

She threw her head back and cackled loudly. It was terrifying—the gooseflesh rising from Alex’s skin was evidence enough of that—but also a bit affected, as though Natacha had watched *The Wizard of Oz* one time too many and practiced her cackle in the mirror.

Suddenly, he felt an iron grip around his wrist.

“I have a bone to pick with you, storyteller,” Natacha said, her fingers digging into his flesh. “I thought I had been perfectly hospitable. Yet you tried to escape the first chance you got. That’s not very polite, is it?”

Alex’s stomach clenched. *Here it comes,* he thought, closing his eyes. *Some kind of horrific spell.*

Natacha released his wrist.

“I’ll let it pass this time,” she said, “on the understanding that you’ve gotten such nonsense out of your system. There’ll be consequences if it happens again. You understand? Say, ‘Yes, Natacha.’”

Alex hesitated as long as he dared.

“Yes, Natacha,” he said, his cheeks flushed with anger.

“Good,” she said.

Natacha pressed the bottom button on the oil diffuser and the machine hummed to life. At first Alex thought that nothing had happened, but then he saw the way that the air shimmered in front of him and reached out a hand.

His fingers touched a solid, invisible wall.

"Four walls," Natacha said. She pointed up. "And a ceiling, of course. My misting room." She pressed the top button on the oil diffuser and blue mist issued from the tiny hole, taking the shape of the invisible room. Alex thought of a fish tank filled with blue-tinged air instead of water.

Natacha inhaled deeply.

What is that stuff? Alex wondered.

"I see you've got a rebellious streak to you," she said, the walls of the misting room muffling her words the slightest bit. "Yasmin here did as well, but now she and I have come to an understanding. She knows better than to even think about crossing me. Isn't that right, Yasmin?"

"Yes, Natacha," the girl said without hesitation.

Natacha turned to him and smiled. Alex thought it was how a cobra might smile if equipped with lips and two full rows of teeth.

"You'll feel the same, in time," she said. "Though I have to confess that I am a *little* disappointed. I thought you might like it here from the start. After all, haven't I given you exactly what you most desire?"

"What are you talking about?" Alex asked.

Natacha laughed at his confused expression.

"Come now, storyteller," she said. "You can lie to me, but don't lie to yourself. I watched you carefully while you were reading your story last night. You loved having an appreciative audience. I could see it on your face. You didn't look like a boy who had lost his freedom. You looked like a boy who had found it."

"All I want to do is go home," Alex said.

"I'm sure you do," Natacha said. "And yet . . . I bet there's a part of you that's been looking forward to telling me a story all day. You probably already picked one out, didn't you?"

Alex wanted to deny it, but he could tell from Natacha's smug smile that the truth was written on his face.

"So what?" he asked. "I wanted to make sure you liked it."

"Because you enjoy the attention, like I said. My guess is that you never share these wonderful nightmares you've set to paper. Are you afraid of what people might think? A young boy with such a hideous imagination?"

"You don't know anything about me," he said, his face burning.

"Then teach me," Natacha said. "Let's start with something simple. Why did you sneak out in the middle of the night to destroy your nightbooks?"

"I don't want to talk about that," Alex said.

The witch nodded—*what you want doesn't really matter*—and waited for him to answer. She drummed her long-nailed fingers on the arm of the chair.

"It's not important," he said.

Clickclick, clickclick.

"Why do you even care?"

Clickclick, clickclick.

Alex could see that Natacha was starting to lose patience. He didn't want to tell her everything, but staying completely silent was not an option. There would be consequences.

Tell her the truth, he thought. *Just not the whole truth.*

"I wanted to be normal," he said. "I didn't want to be Alex Mosher anymore, that fat geeky kid who knows how to make fake blood and can name all the actors who played Michael Myers in the *Halloween* movies. I wanted to fit in, be like other kids, and I thought that destroying my nightbooks would be a step in the right direction. I spent so much time on those stories. I love them with all my heart. I didn't want to destroy them. I *needed* to. That was the only way I could prove to myself that I was serious about changing."

Alex glanced in Yasmin's direction and saw her staring at him with a thoughtful expression. As soon as their eyes met she looked away.

"Alex, Alex, Alex," Natacha said. "Destroying a few notebooks isn't going to change what you are. You have darkness running through your veins, just like me." She settled back in her seat and took a deep breath of the blue mist. "Now spin me a tale," she said. "And this time, make it scary."

MR. BOOTS

Mr. Boots was a white teddy bear with little red boots. Tom brought him everywhere. He pushed Mr. Boots on the swing in his backyard. He held Mr. Boots close during the scary parts of his TV shows. At night when he was supposed to be sleeping, Tom whispered in Mr. Boots's ear. Sometimes Mr. Boots whispered back.

Years passed. Tom got older, and Mr. Boots moved from his bed to his bookshelf. There were new things to play with. A basketball. An iPad. A 3DS. Then bad things started to happen. Tom went to use the iPad one day and saw that the screen was cracked. He woke up and found his 3DS drowned in a sink full of water.

Each time a toy broke, Tom would find Mr. Boots on his bed instead of the bookshelf. It was like the teddy bear hoped that Tom would remember him again, now that his new toy was gone. Tom started to grow suspicious. Except a teddy bear couldn't break an iPad. It couldn't fill a bathroom sink with water.

That was crazy.

Then one day, Tom heard his new basketball hissing air and found a gash made with something sharp. When Mr. Boots appeared in Tom's bed the next morning, his tiny red boots were splattered with mud, as though he had been outside in the backyard. Where the basketball was.

Tom decided enough was enough.

He threw the teddy bear in the garbage.

The next morning Mr. Boots was back in Tom's bed again. He smelled like banana peels and coffee grounds.

Now Tom was scared. He knew he couldn't tell his parents what was going on. They would never believe him. And so he waited until their family vacation. It was a sunny place so far away that they needed to take a plane to get there. Tom brought Mr. Boots. And on the last day of vacation, he buried him in the sand.

This time, Mr. Boots didn't come back.

After a while, Tom forgot all about the stuffed animal. He figured it had just been his imagination. Eventually he moved away from home and went to college. There he met a girl. They got married and had a son named Oliver.

One snowy night, Tom woke up because he thought he heard whispering from Oliver's room. Giggles. Tom didn't think much of it. Oliver was an imaginative child, just as he had been. Tom went back to sleep.

The next morning, Oliver was gone.

Tom and his wife searched the house, but he was nowhere to be found. Finally, they went outside. In the freshly fallen snow, they could see their son's footprints leading into the nearby woods. Next to them were a set of far smaller footprints, the kind made with little red boots.

They never saw Oliver again.

They sat in silence until the blue mist came to a sputtering stop. Natacha breathed in the last of it. The walls of the misting room vanished on their own, leaving behind the strangely sweet smell of gingerbread cookies.

"I like the ending of that one," Natacha said. "It's so *hopeless.*"

"Umm . . . thanks."

"You write that whole thing today?"

Alex started to nod—he wanted Natacha to think that he was working hard—but then stopped himself. He had thought of an idea.

If I phrase this just right, maybe I can get the library all to myself. . . .

"Actually, I wrote that story last year," Alex said. "I meant to read you a new one tonight—something really special—but I couldn't write a single word all day."

Natacha straightened in her seat.

"Why not?" she asked. "Isn't my library good enough for you?"

"It's beautiful. A perfect place to write." Alex hesitated, as though reluctant to tattle on a friend. "It's just . . . You know what, it doesn't matter."

"Out with it!" Natacha exclaimed. "What's the problem?"

Alex blew out a breath, as though Natacha had convinced him to share something that he was planning to keep to himself.

"It's really hard to concentrate with someone staring at me," he said. "I can't write anything at all."

Natacha leaned forward in her seat and pointed a single finger at Yasmin. The girl shook her head, too terrified to speak.

"I told you specifically to show the boy the library and then get out of his way!"

"Not Yasmin!" Alex exclaimed. "She's been very helpful. Seriously—there's no reason to get mad at her. I was talking about Lenore."

Natacha lowered her finger. Yasmin relaxed and glanced at Alex with the slightest hint of gratitude.

"Ah!" said Natacha, chuckling. "Let's see what we can do about that. Get over here, you mangy beast!"

Lenore appeared at the witch's feet. She was already cringing, as though some kind of punishment was a foregone conclusion.

"It's really okay," Alex said, suddenly afraid for the orange cat. "Honestly, I hardly know she's there at—"

The witch raised her hand and Lenore rocketed into the air, her long tail extended straight toward the ceiling as though it were being yanked by an invisible hand. The cat thrashed wildly, hissing in pain.

"Why were you disturbing our storyteller?" Natacha asked when the cat had risen to eye level. "It's very important that he write those stories. *Very* important. You understand me?"

"It wasn't her fault," Alex said. "Stop hurting her!"

Natacha snapped her fingers and Lenore plummeted to the ground. She managed to land on all four paws and ran out of the room.

"That old beast won't bother you anymore," Natacha said. "Now you can write until your hand falls off." She held his gaze and smiled without warmth. "No more excuses, storyteller."

7

THE GIRL WHO FOLLOWED A UNICORN

Alex woke up early the next morning. He found some clean clothes about his own size hanging in the closet and knocked on Yasmin's door. No one answered. Alex figured that she had already passed through the coat closet door and started her work for the day.

What is Natacha making her do? Alex wondered, remembering the scratches along Yasmin's arms, her dirt-stained face. *Something messy, for sure. Digging holes? Burying the bodies of Natacha's victims?* The girl was so confusing. She seemed set on disliking him, but if she hadn't helped Alex that first night, he'd probably be dead.

She's not bad, like Natacha, Alex thought. *She's just scared. Like me.*

He went into the kitchen to grab some breakfast and saw Lenore lying on the counter. She looked away, refusing to acknowledge his presence.

"Sorry about yesterday," Alex said. "I just wanted the library to myself. If I had known that Natacha was going to hurt you, I wouldn't have said anything."

Lenore didn't open her eyes. *Does she even understand what I'm saying?* He knew that Lenore could somehow communicate with Natacha, but maybe that was a witch thing. *Just because she can turn herself invisible doesn't mean she understands English.* Still, he wanted to make it up to her somehow, and since a verbal apology wasn't doing the trick, he grabbed a handful of Froot Loops and spread them on the counter next to her.

"Here," he said. "Maybe this will make you feel—"

Lenore opened her eyes and hissed. Alex saw claws beginning to extend from her paw and jerked his hand backward, but he wasn't nearly fast enough; an orange streak blurred in his direction. Instead of the expected pain, however, Alex felt only a weak patter against his chest. He looked down in confusion and saw Froot Loops falling to the floor.

Lenore had thrown them.

Alex examined her paw more carefully and saw that what he had at first mistaken for claws were actually four tiny fingers and a thumb, covered by a thin layer of black fur. As he watched, these fingers quickly retracted into her paw.

"You're just full of surprises, aren't you?" Alex asked, stunned.

Lenore gave a long, toothy yawn and turned her back to him completely.

Alex retrieved his newest nightbook—the only one with any blank pages left—then used the bonekey that Yasmin had left on the dining room table to enter the library. He spread the nightbook across the desk and laid a pencil next to it.

"There," he said, taking stock, "that looks convincing."

Alex had no intention of actually trying to write a story, but now if Natacha entered the library unannounced he could at least *look* like he had been working. For the time being, he would just claim that his old stories were actually new ones.

I haven't written many in this nightbook yet, Alex thought, *but there has to be over fifty stories between the two older ones. If all I'm doing is reading one story a night, I have plenty of time. Right now it's more important to learn as much about the apartment as possible so I can figure out a way to escape.*

Alex had always relied on books to be his teachers. Hoping that things would be no different here, he set out to explore the library. *Yasmin said these were all story collections,* he thought, *but what if she was wrong? What if there's something here that I can use?* He scanned the titles. *The Black Horseshoe and Other Tales of Equine Horror. Stories Scratched Beneath a Coffin Lid. 13 Dead Ends.* Alex would have loved to read them all, but other than entertainment value he didn't think they would be of much use. Then again, what exactly was he looking for? *A spell book could be helpful,* he thought. *Or, even better, one of those fake books that unlocks a secret passageway leading out of this place.*

Alex didn't see anything like that. All he saw were storybooks.

As he made his way up the winding staircase, the books grew older, the dust jackets giving way to leather bindings cracked with age. English faded from the spines, gradually replaced by what Alex thought was German. "*Der Dunkle Wald,*" he read hesitantly, tripping over the foreign words. "*Das Buch der Verlorenen Kinder.*" With no other way to tell what kind of books these were, Alex flipped through one at random, his gaze lingering on several woodcuts: a beautiful woman sleeping in a casket made of glass; a grotesque imp dancing in delight around a campfire; an old crone leading a boy and girl into a house made of candy.

Fairy tales, Alex thought, closing the book. *The original scary stories.*

By the time he finally reached the top of the tower, Alex was panting from exertion. He stretched his hand into the air and grazed the stone ceiling with the tips of his fingers. It was as solid as expected. Alex hadn't really believed that there would be an exit at the top of the staircase, but he was disappointed nevertheless.

"Now what?" he asked.

The titles were clearly a dead end. Yet Alex, who felt that libraries possessed their own sort of magic, still believed that there was something important to be learned here. *I need to search the books themselves,* he thought. *At the very least, I can see what type of story Natacha likes. That could be helpful, if I ever do have to write some new ones.*

Alex quickly retraced his path—a little bit easier than going up, but not by much—and grabbed the first five books off the lowest shelf. There were other titles that seemed more interesting, but Alex figured the best way to perform a thorough search was to start at the beginning and methodically work his way upward. He sat down at his writing desk and tucked four of the books beneath his chair, where they would remain hidden if he had any unexpected visitors.

Stay focused, he warned himself, knowing that once he started reading, he might get distracted and forget the main purpose of his search.

Alex opened the first book.

It was a volume dedicated to ghost stories. Alex tried to skim, he really did, but every so often a turn of phrase would bait his eye and he would forget himself for several pages before breaking through the surface again and remembering his task. The next book, a collection of poorly written urban legends, wasn't nearly as interesting. Alex was able to give it a cursory examination in less than ten minutes. He set it at the bottom of the pile and placed the third book on the table, a quartet of creepy novellas titled *Handprints on the Window.*

It was long. Really long.

Alex braced himself with a single elbow and flipped through the pages, for the first time feeling the enormity of his task.

Am I wasting my time with this? he wondered. *Maybe I should pull each book off the shelf and check to see if there's something behind them. . . .*

Lost in his doubts, it took Alex an extra beat to realize that there was something different about this book. When he finally saw it, he had to flip back a couple of pages to where the change first began.

There was writing in the margins.

Words huddled together in small groups. They had been printed with a pencil; here and there Alex could even see erasure marks where the writer had made a correction. The penmanship wasn't the neatest, but it was legible enough.

It looks like it was written by a kid, Alex thought. *Maybe someone my age.*

He started to read.

Shh! I told the witch that I'm in here picking tonight's story for her. But I want to write some things down first. I don't have any paper so I'm going to use these books. Different book each time. So the witch don't find out. If she does I'll be in BIG TROUBLE!

How I got here was I was playing in the park and saw a unicorn walk into this apartmen building.

Raymond was awoken in the middle of the night by scratching noises on the other side of his bedroom ceiling. He lay in bed and listened carefully. Something scampered from one side of the ceiling to the other, a trail of sound.

"Mouse," Raymond muttered in disgust. He had lived alone in the old farmhouse for over sixty years, and it wasn't the first time a rodent had tried to use his attic for a winter home. Well, I'm up now, *he thought.* Might as well get some traps up there before I have an infestation on my hands.

I know unicorns aren't real. I'm not stupid.

He dressed quickly and started a pot of coffee. The scratching noise continued, louder than before. Raymond reassessed his earlier opinion. Could be a squirrel, *he thought.* Maybe even a raccoon. *He pulled down the attic stairs and climbed them carefully, his arthritic knees barking in protest. Sunrise was still a few hours away, and the attic was cold*

But I have always LOVED LOVED LOVED unicorns so I followed it anyway. Just in case. It went into the elevato which is funny! And I took the stairs and saw it walk into this apartment. I knocked on the door and the witch who lives here trapped me inside. ⟶ And so here I am.

now Mom and Dad will find me ry soon. I just have to do what the tch tells me to do. She won't hurt e. I am a ood girl.

and dark. Raymond ducked his head beneath the low ceiling and shone a flashlight to the left and right, where the spaces between the joists remained exposed. He was looking for rips in the insulation, some kind of sign that he had an unwelcome guest.

Instead, he found a strange lump about the size of a softball.

Plus she can do magic which I think is SO COOL.

is lonely too. Otherwise why does she want someone to read her a story every night?

"What is that?" he asked.

Raymond slowly got to his knees and parted the fiberglass insulation with his shirtsleeves, revealing a silver, oval-shaped object speckled with red dots. An egg, Raymond thought, struggling to come to terms with the sheer strangeness of it. Some kind of bird get in here, maybe? *He swung his flashlight over the rest of the insulation and saw similar lumps evenly spaced throughout the attic: a dozen, maybe two.*

Also her cat can turn invisible!!!!....

The silver egg shook.

Raymond fell backward in surprise, his hand connecting with something warm and slimy on the floor. It slithered between his fingers and underneath the sleeve of his shirt, moving fast.

And also also I think there were other kids here but they are not here anymore so the witch must have let them go. If I am a good girl she will

The writing stopped in midsentence. Alex could imagine the girl hearing footsteps in the distance and slipping the book back onto the shelf. He flipped through the rest of the pages, but there was nothing more.

Alex stared down at the book, trying to process all that he had learned. A sheen of cold sweat gathered at the nape of his neck.

Could Yasmin have written this? he wondered—and quickly rejected the possibility. It didn't sound like her at all, and Yasmin was far too frightened of the witch to deface one of her precious storybooks. *It must have been another prisoner. Before me and Yasmin.* Alex stared up at the library. *I have to keep searching and see if she wrote more in a different book. She might have learned something important! She might have escaped!*

Before Alex could get out of his seat, however, he heard the familiar clicking sound of a bonekey turning in the lock. He slipped the book of novellas beneath his desk and grabbed a pencil, trying to look as though he had been dutifully at work this entire time.

The door opened.

8

BEAUTIFUL DARKNESS

"Hey," Yasmin said, stepping into the room.

"Hey," Alex said, as naturally as possible.

Yasmin's goggles hung around her neck. There were fresh scratches on her arm. Her apron was splattered with some yellow, viscous substance.

She shook the dirt out of her hair and slipped the Mets cap on her head.

"Dinner will be ready in like an hour," she said, "so you should finish up whatever you're doing."

"Thanks," Alex said.

"Okay, then." She turned around as if to leave, and then turned back. "That story you read last night? It didn't suck."

Alex looked down at the desk so Yasmin didn't see the blush spreading across his face.

"You really think so?" he asked.

She gave him a strange look.

"This can't be the first time someone said you're a good writer. Your English teacher must love you."

"Not exactly," Alex said. "I do okay in school with essays and stuff, but it's not the same. And I've never shared my nightbook stories before."

"Is it like you said yesterday?" Yasmin asked. "You afraid people will think you're weird?"

He nodded.

"Well, you don't have to worry about that happening with me," Yasmin said. "I already think you're weird. You can't make it any worse."

"Thanks," Alex said, unable to tell from her stone-faced expression if she was joking or not. *Maybe that's just the way she is,* he thought. *This might be an attempt to befriend me.* If so, Alex couldn't mess it up. He needed Yasmin's help if he wanted to escape the apartment.

Unfortunately, the girl was already turning to go. To keep the conversation alive, Alex asked the first question that popped into his head.

"Did you live here, in the building? You know, before?"

Yasmin gave a quick shake of her head.

"Then how did you get here?" Alex asked.

"I don't like to talk about it, okay?"

She left the library and headed toward the kitchen.

"That's cool," Alex said. He held the door open as he

called after her. "I was just curious how Natacha tricked you into coming inside. With me it was a scary movie."

Yasmin stopped and looked back over one shoulder.

"What does that even mean?" she asked.

"I heard it playing behind the apartment door," Alex said. "It called to me. I couldn't stop myself from knocking."

"A movie?" she asked in disbelief. "*That's* how Natacha got you?"

"It wasn't my fault," Alex said, growing angry. "Magic, remember? It brainwashed me."

"Whatever."

"Well, how did you get trapped, then?" Alex asked. He looked at her cap and scoffed. "Let me guess. You heard the Mets playing on TV. Ninth inning. And you just couldn't help yourself."

Her expression grew cold.

"You want to know what happened?" she asked, stepping forward. "Fine. My friend Amena lives in this apartment building. On the twelfth floor. Only when I came to see her that Saturday, the elevator stopped on the fourth. Weird, but no big deal, right? I get off the elevator, thinking I'll just take the stairs, when I smell the most amazing thing. *Kusa mihshi.*" Yasmin registered Alex's confused look and added, "That's rice and lamb—or chickpeas, if you're a vegetarian like me—all mashed together inside squash, cooked with lemon juice, mint, and a ton of garlic."

"Sounds delicious," Alex said, stomach grumbling.

"It is," replied Yasmin. Her voice softened. "My sito—grandma—and I used to make it together. As soon as I smelled it, I ran down the hallway, no longer thinking straight. I was convinced that if I knocked on the door to apartment 4E, Sito would answer." Yasmin looked away. "She didn't, of course. How could she? My sito's been dead for over a year. But for that one moment, I was positive that she had been returned to me. And then, finding out it was all a trick? It was like losing her all over again."

For a few moments, Alex didn't know what to say.

"I'm sorry," he finally managed.

Yasmin wiped away the tears that had begun to fall from her eyes.

"So what was the movie?" she asked.

"What?"

"The one you heard through the apartment door."

"Oh," Alex said, wishing that he had never brought it up in the first place. "*Night of the Living Dead*."

Yasmin shrugged her shoulders.

"Never heard of it."

She turned and left. This time, she didn't look back.

After dinner, Natacha set up the oil diffuser and settled into her chair. Alex took his place next to her. Despite everything, he was excited to read the story he had picked out.

Natacha's right, he thought. *I do love an appreciative audience.*

"You able to work better without that disgusting fur ball in the room?" she asked.

"Yes," Alex said. "Thank you."

"This can be a good home for you, storyteller," Natacha said as Yasmin took her place on the love seat and primly folded her hands in her lap. "A place where you can be yourself. I was thinking about what you told me yesterday, how you wanted to sacrifice your poor little nightbooks so you could be as boring as other children your age. I'm curious about something. Being different isn't anything new for you, is it? Truly, you've been blessed with these dark thoughts your entire life." She leaned forward and clasped her hands beneath her chin. "So why the sudden change of heart? What happened?"

Alex almost told her, but his storytelling instincts again warned him that it would be best to keep the real story of the nightbooks to himself. The witch wouldn't hurt him, because if she did, she'd never find out the truth.

Just like Scheherazade, he thought.

"Nothing specific happened," Alex said. "It was just time for a change."

"Is that so?" asked Natacha.

She smirked, clearly seeing through his lie but allowing it to pass for now. The meaning in her haughty expression was clear: *You'll tell me eventually. It's not like you're going anywhere.*

"I left you fresh paper in the library," she said, eyeing the nightbook in his hand. "Why are you still using that old thing?"

"Just used to it, I guess," Alex said.

"Give it here."

She flicked her wrist and the book flew into her hands. Alex jumped in surprise and Natacha cackled heartily.

"That was a good spell, no?"

"Amazing," Alex said, when it was clear that she was waiting for a response. Compared to creating magical rooms that bent the laws of reality, making a book fly into your hand was pretty small potatoes. Nevertheless, Natacha seemed immensely impressed with herself. Apparently Alex wasn't the only one who enjoyed an audience.

She turned the nightbook in her hands.

"What happened here?" she asked, examining the outside of the book. The back and front covers had peeled away in several sections, exposing raw strips of white. Only a rubber band kept the loose pages from slipping away. "You have a temper tantrum when writing wasn't going your way?"

Alex hesitated, not wanting to tell Natacha any more about himself than necessary. When her eyes narrowed, however, he began to talk.

"That started as my writing journal when I was in the fourth grade," he said. "My teacher told us to cover it with pictures of things we liked, so the journals would be more personalized. I went online and printed out all my favorite things: zombies, monsters, killer dolls . . . it was really hard to fit them all on the notebook, but I worked at it, cutting each picture exactly right so it all fit together like a puzzle. Took me the entire weekend, but it was worth it. I couldn't wait to start writing." The smile that had blossomed on Alex's face suddenly faded. "And then I brought it to school. I saw how different mine was from everyone else's. They had all printed out pictures of athletes, cute animals, boy bands, photos of friends and family. We had to leave the notebooks out on our desk that first day, like a museum, and the other kids kept staring at mine and giving me weird looks. I took the journal home that night and tore all the pictures off. It became my first nightbook."

Natacha stared at him for a long time and sighed deeply.

"I am all kinds of mystified by you, boy," she said. "The beautiful darkness that dances through your brain is a cause for celebration! And yet, for some strange reason, you run from it. Why is that?"

"I just want to be like everyone else," Alex said.

Natacha laughed.

"What makes you think you have a choice?" she asked. She handed him the nightbook and pressed a button on the oil diffuser. The air shimmered as the misting room came into being. "You're not like everyone else, and there's nothing you can do about it! We are what we are. These stories, they're just the real you bubbling to the surface: weird and dark and twisted."

Alex felt his face growing warm. Natacha was saying everything that he had always feared.

She's right, he thought. *There's darkness running through me. Why else would I have all these terrible ideas in my—*

"Oh, goodness," Natacha said, her face cloaked by blue mist. "Now you're all sad and misty-eyed. Hey—you know what always cheers me up? A story. So get to it."

THE SHAPE IN THE MIRROR

Katie loved vampires. She had read all the books and watched all the movies. She knew all the rules. A vampire couldn't enter a house without being invited first. They didn't cast a reflection. You became a vampire by getting bitten or drinking vampire blood. Sometimes Katie thought it would be cool to be a vampire. She made the mistake of telling this to some kids at lunch. They decided that Katie was weird and started to bully her. It spread like wildfire throughout the school. It got so bad that Katie and her family had to move to a different town.

Their new house wasn't as nice as their old house. There was a musty smell that wouldn't go away no matter how many times her parents scrubbed the floors. Even weirder, the former occupants had abandoned some of their furniture, as though they had left in a hurry. An old sofa. Several bookcases.

The mirror in Katie's room.

It was really old, with strange symbols carved into the wooden frame. Katie's dad offered to move it to the basement, but Katie told him no. She liked creepy things.

The next morning, Katie saw something unusual.

Her room was on the first floor, and the way the mirror was turned you could look into it and see through her bedroom window all the way to the house across the street. Behind her reflection, she saw a dark shape in her neighbors' front yard. Katie turned around and peeked through her window, thinking that it must be a dog or something. The front lawn was empty. When Katie looked back in the mirror, however, she could see the shape again. In fact, she thought it had gotten a little closer.

She checked again.

Through the window? No shape.

In the mirror? Shape.

It was impossible! Katie called her big brother to show him, but the shape had completely vanished. Her brother shook his head and called her a freakazoid like he always did. He missed his friends and blamed Katie for the sudden move.

The shape didn't appear for three more days. When it finally returned, there was no doubt that it had gotten closer. Instead of sitting on her neighbors' front lawn, the shape had crossed to the middle of the street. Katie still couldn't tell what it was. The reflection was blurry, as though that part of the mirror was smudged. She thought it might have been some kind of animal.

Katie didn't see the shape for a very long time after that.

Eventually she figured that it had all just been a figment of her imagination. But then she looked in the mirror one night and saw the shape peeking through her window. She could see it clearly now. It had bat-like wings folded around its body like a black robe and eyes as red as blood. A single claw reached up and scratched the glass.

Katie covered the mirror with a blanket.

She told her parents what she had seen. They exchanged a worried glance and said they would get rid of the mirror first thing in the morning. Her father told Katie to sleep in the guest room. She was trying to do just that when her brother walked in. He said that he had overheard their parents talking. They didn't believe that there was really a shape in the mirror. They thought Katie was crazy and tomorrow some men in white coats were going to come and take her away forever.

Katie decided that there was only one way to prove that she was telling the truth so her parents didn't send her away. When she was sure that everyone was asleep, she snuck up to her room and pulled the blanket off the mirror.

The shape was standing right behind her reflection.

Its ancient, scrunched-up face was covered by a thin layer of fur. It reached down and wrapped its long talons around mirror Katie. Then it unfurled its massive wings and rose out of sight, taking the reflection with it.

Katie stared into the mirror. She saw nothing but the empty room behind her. The shape was gone. Her reflection was gone.

She fainted.

Katie woke up the next morning hating sunlight. By nighttime, two long fangs had punched through her upper gums. It turned out that she wasn't such a vampire expert after all. She had always thought that people lost their reflection after they became vampires. Now she knew it was the other way around. First your reflection was stolen. Then the change began.

Her stomach rumbled.

Katie crept down the hallway to her brother's bedroom. He was asleep. His head was turned away from her, exposing his bare neck.

She entered his room and closed the door behind her.

Alex finished reading just as the oil diffuser's cycle came to an end. Blue mist dispersed into the air as the magical walls vanished.

"Your story is all wrong," Natacha said.

Alex's cheeks burned.

"What do you mean?" he asked, unable to meet her eyes. This was part of the reason why he never shared his stories with anyone else. The slightest criticism was a hornet's sting.

"The girl, she turns into a vampire at the end, right?"

"Right."

"But that can't be! She never gets bitten by one!"

"That's the whole idea," Alex said, hating the defensive tone in his voice. "I wanted to do something different, so I made the mirror creature turn her into a vampire by taking her reflection."

"But that's not how it *works*," Natacha said in a petulant tone. "I'm surprised at you, storyteller. I thought you knew better than that."

Alex considered arguing, but he could see that it wouldn't do any good. Natacha would never understand that he was trying to do something creative. In her mind, the story had simply been inaccurate.

"Sorry," Alex said.

"Apology accepted," replied Natacha. She smiled smugly,

like a know-it-all who had just proved the teacher wrong. "Fortunately for you, I'm a witch, which makes me an expert in these matters. I'll be sure to let you know if you get any other details wrong in the future."

"Can't wait," Alex muttered under his breath.

Natacha stood up and pressed her ear against a wall. After a few moments, she nodded with satisfaction.

"Good news," she said. "Your story might not have made any sense, but it still got the job done."

Alex's face flushed, this time with anger instead of embarrassment. He was tired of hearing his writing criticized.

"What do you mean, 'got the job done'?" he snapped, ignoring Yasmin's look of warning. "What are you even listening to?"

Natacha gave him an appraising look.

"One of those, are you?" she asked, rubbing her hands together. "Curious type? Got to know what makes the clock tick? The rain fall? Not so fond of that characteristic, Alex. Leads to trouble."

Alex swallowed nervously as Natacha took a step closer to him.

"Sorry," he said. "I just . . . thought it might make a good story, you know. Noises in the walls. Creepy stuff."

"Always the little author," Natacha said, though it was

clear by the look on her face that she didn't believe him. "You're sure you're not curious about the apartment itself? Maybe you think you could figure out a way to escape, if only you knew its secrets?"

"No," Alex said. "It's not like that at—"

Natacha snapped her fingers in his face. Alex flinched, expecting a spell, but she just wanted him to stop talking.

"Since you're being so forthcoming with me," Natacha said, spitting out the word *forthcoming* in a way that implied its opposite, "I'll do the same for you. The dark magic that keeps this apartment up and running is very old and not quite what it used to be. Sometimes things shift out of alignment and grind together, like a car that's been driven too many miles. When that happens, the walls shake. Cracks appear."

Alex nodded, remembering his first day in the apartment, how he thought he was in the middle of an earthquake.

"The thing about dark magic, though—it thrives on nightmares," Natacha said. "When you read it a scary story, you soothe its aches and pains. And then it can rest easy again—at least for a little while."

Alex watched Natacha carefully as she spoke. The smirk on her face made it clear that she was keeping something from him, and that she wanted him to know that she was keeping something from him. She was teasing him with half-truths.

"Are you saying the apartment is alive?" Alex asked.

Natacha snorted with laughter.

"Now that's a crazy idea," she said. "Maybe you can write a story about it."

9

WHAT GROWS WITH NO LIGHT

Alex's new life in apartment 4E settled into a predictable routine.

During the day, he pretended to write in the library while combing the stacks for another entry written by the mysterious girl. It was slow going. Not only did Alex need to examine every page of every book, but he kept getting distracted by the stories themselves, often losing himself in reading for hours on end.

It was the only way he could escape the apartment.

At night, Alex read aloud while Natacha sat in her misting room (she didn't offer any more information about the purpose of the blue mist, and Alex didn't ask—though he did develop a theory). After each story the witch listened to the wall for a moment and then patted it like an obedient steed. Alex didn't completely buy her explanation about the dark magic of the apartment being appeased by his narrative offerings, but he kept these doubts to himself. No good could come of questioning her. Besides, he *liked* sharing his stories. Maybe Natacha was overly fond of correcting him, especially if the story contained any magic, but at least Alex didn't have to worry about the witch thinking he was a freak for having such a dark imagination. As Natacha said again and again, they were one and the same.

The same darkness that runs through Natacha's veins runs through my own, Alex thought.

It scared him.

Alex wished he could talk to Yasmin about all of this—and share his exciting discovery in the library—but she continued to spurn his attempts at friendship. Eventually he gave up, and they each settled into their section of the apartment: Alex in the library, Yasmin in the place behind the coat closet door. They barely exchanged a word all day.

Alex grew lonely with only his thoughts to keep him company. These inevitably turned to his family.

He missed them so much.

Days were bad. Nights were worse. The fact that his family was only four floors away didn't make him feel any better. They might as well have been on Saturn.

Sometimes he imagined their reunion, playing it in his head like the end of a cheesy movie. *I knock on our apartment door. Mom and Dad answer. They don't hug me at first. They're in shock. They can't believe it's really their son, safe and sound. And then it starts: the tears, the hugs, the kisses. Even John gives me an affectionate fist tap.*

Alex longed to make this fantasy a reality. There was only one way to do it.

Escape.

He wished he could search the apartment more thoroughly to see if he had missed a clue, but it was impossible. Lenore could be anywhere. Besides, if there *was* an exit, he knew exactly where it would be.

Through Natacha's bedroom door.

Alex doubted that there was anything special about the actual bedroom itself; his interest was in the magical room accessed by the bonekey. He had only seen Natacha enter this way once, and she had checked around carefully before slipping the bonekey inside, shooing Alex away when she saw him standing at the end of the hallway.

Whatever was behind that door was so important that she didn't want Alex catching a single glimpse.

He was dying to know what it was, just like he was dying to know what Yasmin did in the coat closet each day. Unfortunately, the only way to find out was to steal Natacha's bonekeys, which she kept in her pocket at all times. Alex wasn't desperate enough to try something *that* crazy. Not yet, at least.

Days passed. Alex searched the library. Told his stories. Dreamed of escape.

He imagined that things would have continued in this fashion if it hadn't been for the danglers.

Alex had been combing the stacks all morning with nothing to show for it but blurry eyes and an aching back. He cleaned his glasses on the bottom of his shirt while considering the number of books waiting to be searched. Even after a week, he had barely made a dent.

This is going to take forever, he thought.

He had found, to this point, exactly six other entries by the mystery writer, who he had dubbed Unicorn Girl. As far as Alex could tell, she had shelved the books at random, and as there were no dates to tell him their precise chronological order, he relied instead upon the rising desperation in their tone. Thus the earliest two entries, Alex believed, were drawings of unicorns, little more than cheerful graffiti in the margins. The next one was a list:

Things I Miss
Mom
Dad
ICE CREAM!!!
Jude (sometimes)
Raindrops

Alex, whose mind often wandered to his life before the apartment, knew exactly how Unicorn Girl felt. He also thought it was funny how she put Jude (who he assumed was her brother) after ice cream. It made him feel like he knew her a little bit.

The fourth entry, on the other hand, just made him sad. Five sentences formed a heart around a carefully rendered sketch of a unicorn pendant:

> My special pin. From Mom + Dad. I wear it close to my heart and touch it when I need to remember them better. When they get fuzzy in my brain. I will NEVER EVER NEVER take it off!!!

"Fuzzy in my brain"? Alex wondered. *Does that mean she's starting to forget her parents? How long has she been Natacha's prisoner at this point?*

According to the fifth entry, even Unicorn Girl didn't know:

> Today I tried to figure out how long I been here. Couldn't. The days and nights get all mixed up. I asked the witch how long but she wouldn't tell me. The witch don't tell me nothing. She just wants her story every night. I'm so tired of reading her scary stories.
>
> I HATE HER.

I've been looking for a spell book. Thinking if I could do magic then I could make her pay. But the only books here are stories. Stupid useless stories.

I seen a movie where this guy with a big beard made scratches in a prison wall so he could remember how long he'd been there. I should have done that. Except I never thought it would be this long. And now it's too late to start.

Just thinking about this entry depressed him. When Unicorn Girl had first been captured, she believed that Natacha was a lonely woman who would eventually set her free. That hope and optimism was gone now. She had changed.

Is that what's going to happen to me? Alex wondered.

He hoped not. And if the final entry was any indication, maybe he could avoid such a fate:

I escape tonight. Everything is set.

I escape tonight, Alex thought, the three simple words quickening his heart. *Everything is set. That means she had a plan.* If so, it was entirely conceivable that she wrote it down. The answer that Alex sought might be waiting somewhere in the library.

It was great news. *Spectacular* news.

If Unicorn Girl had really written her plan down, and *if* he could find it.

He had the sneaking suspicion that it wasn't going to happen today. He considered taking a break from his search and reading for a while—a slim volume titled *The Maze Inside the Labyrinth* had caught his eye—but instead sat at the table and opened his nightbook.

I should try to write something, he thought. *Just in case Natacha starts getting suspicious.*

This nightbook—the one with the peeling cover—was the only one he had used since coming to apartment 4E. He had already read most of the stories, but Alex wasn't worried. He still had the two other nightbooks in his backpack. Last night he had flipped through them, just to see what was there. Some of the stories had been written when he was only eight or nine, and Alex didn't think that they were good enough to share. Others were little more than unfinished ideas that had fizzled out like defective fireworks. Even excluding those, however, Alex still had over forty stories in the bank.

That's plenty for now, he thought, closing the nightbook. *No need to worry about it.*

There was a knock at the door.

Alex pushed his chair back, unsure who it could be. When Yasmin came to tell him that it was dinnertime every night, she simply walked into the library without knocking. And although Natacha had never actually checked on him, Alex doubted that she would be so polite.

Could it be someone else? he thought. *Maybe the apartment lured a new kid inside?*

He inched the door open and peeked cautiously through the gap.

It was Yasmin.

Usually her face was flat and expressionless, as though her emotions were a secret she wanted to keep hidden from the world. Today, however, Yasmin was visibly upset. She rocked back and forth on her heels while twisting the bottom of her T-shirt into a knot.

"I need your help," she said.

"With what?" Alex asked.

"I . . . something happened . . . and . . ."

Yasmin pulled the brim of her Mets cap tight over her forehead and closed her eyes, as though trying to wish the entire situation away.

"This is a mistake," she said, wrapping her arms around herself. "I'm sure I can figure out a way . . . to fix it on my own. I shouldn't expect you to . . . to . . ."

She took a few steps back.

"Yasmin," Alex said. "Let me help. Whatever it is, you

don't have to do it alone."

She stared at him a moment with a dubious expression on her face. Finally, she nodded.

"I'll have to get the extra pair of goggles first," she said. "One of the lenses is cracked, but I think it'll still work."

"Why do I need goggles?"

"To protect your eyes."

"I know what goggles *do*, I meant—"

"And see if you can find a pair of gloves," Yasmin said, cutting him off. "Thick ones."

"What exactly are we doing?" Alex asked.

"It'll be easier to explain once we're inside," Yasmin said. She smiled weakly. "You wanted to know what I do every day, right? Well, you're about to find out."

Once Alex had tracked down two mismatched gloves (one bright pink, the other with a small hole in the left pinkie), he met Yasmin in front of the coat closet door. She handed him a pair of yellow-tinted goggles that looked like something you might wear during science lab. Alex slipped them over his eyes. The band was too tight around his head, but he didn't want to take the time to adjust it. He was afraid that any hesitation might give Yasmin the opportunity to change her mind.

"Let's go," Yasmin said.

"What about her?" Alex asked, nodding his head toward

Lenore. The cat sat in the middle of the living room floor, watching them with interest. She had stayed out of Alex's way since he told Natacha that he needed solitude in order to work, but every so often he caught her staring at him with cold green eyes. The witch already seemed to dislike the cat, and by stripping Lenore of her library duty Alex had diminished her value even further. If she had a chance at redemption, he was certain she would take it.

"Lenore's going to come whether we like it or not," Yasmin said. "It'll be much worse if we try to lock her out. Then Natacha will *really* think we're up to something."

She slid the bonekey into the keyhole and pulled the door open. The expensive coats that normally weighted down the rod were no longer there. Instead, Alex saw an open expanse of darkness, like a cavern. The dimensions were impossibly huge, but he wasn't as fazed by that as he would have been a week ago.

Lenore passed between them and vanished into the murk.

"You can't see anything at the start," Yasmin said. "So just follow my footsteps and try to keep up."

"There's no light at all?" Alex asked.

"Not the kind you're thinking of," she said. "That reminds me, close the door behind you."

Alex didn't like the idea of plunging them into total darkness, so when Yasmin turned around he left the door open a crack. It made him feel a little better, knowing that there was still the slightest thread of light in this place.

"We should have brought a flashlight," he said, following the echo of Yasmin's footsteps.

"That's the last thing you want to do," she said. "Besides, you don't really need it. Just keep walking straight. It's not far. See—you're about to pass through a big curtain here." Her voice was suddenly muffled. "It's on the other side."

Alex, walking through the darkness with hands outstretched, felt something heavy and smooth hanging from the ceiling. It reminded him of those lead aprons that dentists made you wear when they x-rayed your teeth. There was a seam in its center. Alex slipped through it.

And gasped with wonder.

Alex liked to write about things that didn't exist. He saw them clearly enough in his imagination, but in order to paint a picture in the reader's mind he created links to the real world. For that reason, he might describe a monster as a "scaly rat with wings," or compare the smell of a sunbaked zombie to "a liverwurst sandwich left in a locker over summer vacation." The sight before him now was so remarkable, however, that there was nothing on earth with which to compare it. Alex could only describe it in terms of imaginary things: a phosphorescent garden on some alien planet, a neon forest hidden at the center of the earth.

"What is this place?" Alex asked, staring slack-jawed

at the long tables that stretched into the distance. From clay plots and long lacquer boxes grew a dizzying variety of flora whose violent colors exploded in the dark. In some cases, they resembled plants and flowers familiar to Alex. A lily the color of hibiscus tea. Yellow sunflowers like streaks of colored chalk on a blackboard. A tiny cactus, its needles tipped with red.

In most cases, however, the plants were unlike anything that Alex had ever seen.

Some breathed. Some snapped. Some chewed.

The air was filled with the musty smell of growing things but there was something slightly spoiled beneath it all, as though someone had committed a murder and hid the body to rot.

Alex was both exhilarated and afraid.

"It's a nursery," Yasmin said. Her white shirt glowed in the dark, like she was about to play a game of laser tag. "Well, that's what Natacha calls it, at least. Except these aren't normal plants, as you probably noticed. They're meant to grow at night. You put them under direct sunlight, or even a lightbulb, and they'd be dead in an hour. That's why we use black light instead."

Long fluorescent tubes dangled above the tables. They gave off a faint, purplish glow.

"Isn't black light what they use to make bloodstains show up at crime scenes?" Alex asked, remembering something he had read while doing research on forensic investigations for a story.

"Is it?" Yasmin asked. He expected to hear disgust in her voice, just like other kids when his gruesome interests spilled into the conversation, but instead there was only mild interest. "The only time I've ever seen black lights in the real world was at this indoor mini-golf place. All the windmills and golf balls and stuff glowed in the dark. Just like this, except without the magic plants."

"These plants are magic?" Alex asked.

"It's a witch's nursery," Yasmin said. "What did you expect? Geraniums? Come on. We need to hurry."

She set off between the tables, walking at a fast clip. Alex had to practically run to keep up.

"If these plants are magic," he asked, "what do they do?"

"Nothing yet," Yasmin said. "They're just ingredients. You have to put them together the right way for anything to happen."

An electric thrill ran through Alex's body.

"Are you talking about magic potions?" he asked.

"According to Natacha, no one wants potions anymore," Yasmin said. "Customers refuse to put up with the taste. These days it's all essential oils. People put a few drops in these misters, like the kind you use to make the room smell good, and breathe in the magic." She sighed, remembering something. "That reminds me, I have to check the distillers. I started a new batch of wealth oil yesterday."

"You're the one who makes them?" Alex asked in amazement.

"Anyone can do it," Yasmin said, though he thought he detected a hint of pride in her voice. "There's no magic involved. You just have to follow the recipe, like cooking."

"What about the blue oil that Natacha puts in her diffuser?" Alex asked. "Are you the one who—"

"No way," Yasmin said. "I make the harmless stuff. Like, the oil that will give you good luck on a job interview. Natacha's not stupid. She doesn't teach me how to make anything that can hurt her."

"Do you at least know what the blue oil is for?" Alex asked.

Yasmin walked faster, clearly uncomfortable with the change in topic.

"Never really thought about it," she mumbled.

"I have a theory," Alex said, catching up with her. "It's total fairy-tale stuff, but that doesn't mean I'm wrong. Natacha looks like she's what—twenty-eight, thirty? I think she's a lot older than that and it's the blue mist that keeps her young. So many things start to make sense then. The way the apartment is decorated, the furniture, the wallpaper, those creepy little statues of kids—it's like a grandma's house, you know. And all those books in her library? Some of them are *ancient.* I'm sure she's been collecting them for decades, maybe even centuries. . . ."

Yasmin stopped short and turned to face him.

"It's best not to talk about things like this," she said sharply. "It doesn't concern me. Or you."

Her eyes flitted around the room and then settled on Alex, urging him to silence. Finally, he understood.

I forgot about Lenore! She's probably standing nearby, eavesdropping. The little spy will report anything we say about Natacha.

"You're right," Alex said. "It's really none of my business what Natacha does."

Yasmin gave him the slightest nod: *Now you get it.* A tiny surge of joy sparked inside Alex. It felt good to talk to someone without using words. That was something that friends did.

"What did you need my help with?" he asked as they started walking again. He fiddled with his goggles, which were beginning to fog up from the exertion.

"Almost there," Yasmin said. "And don't take your goggles off. The light can really hurt your eyes."

"I'm surprised Natacha cared enough to give you them in the first place."

"She doesn't *care,*" Yasmin said. "I'm just no use to her if I'm blind."

As they moved, Alex glanced over at the long tables,

his eyes jumping from wonder to wonder. Small placards, like you might find in a regular greenhouse, sat in front of each planter:

WIDOW ORCHID.
Mix water with snake venom. Spritz daily.

DEMON'S MANE.
Feed dried tarantula legs when petals are open. Beware of acid.

NIGHTBERRIES.
Plant in soil from freshly dug grave.
Water with a child's tears. Great for baking!

"You take care of all of these plants by yourself?" Alex asked.

"Yup."

"Wow," he said, suddenly feeling guilty for his lazy days spent combing books in the library. "That's a lot of work for one person. How do you keep up?"

"I like to keep busy," Yasmin said. "Always have." She paused to pluck a few needles from an orange herb and slip them in her pocket. "It would be a lot easier if these plants weren't so fragile. Feed them the wrong thing, or at the wrong time, or in the wrong way, and bad things happen. Which is why I brought you here in the first place." She scratched the back of her neck. "I screwed up. Big-time.

I was so tired, and it's hard to read those little signs in front of each plant with these goggles on, and I ended up feeding a snapping vine *rat's* blood instead of *bat's* blood."

"You have both?"

"And cat's blood. There's a whole blood shelf. That's not the point. The point is now the plant is . . . um . . . sick."

"Sick?"

"The good news is I know how to fix it. I'm sure Lenore's going to tell Natacha, one way or the other, but I figure if everything is better already—that should help, at least. Problem is, it isn't something I can fix on my own."

"We'll do it together, then," Alex said.

Yasmin removed her cap in order to fix a few strands of hair that had slipped free. Her face was ashen.

"You're nice," she said. "And I appreciate your help. But this still doesn't change anything. I don't want to be your friend. I don't want any friends. Not anymore."

There was no anger in the words, only sadness. Alex had assumed that Yasmin kept her distance because she thought he was a weirdo. Now he wondered if there was a different reason, something that didn't involve him at all.

Why doesn't she want friends? Alex thought.

He followed Yasmin deeper into the darkness.

10

DANGLERS

They walked between a series of long tables, their way lit by glowing plants. Alex passed a neon-green flower with toothlike petals that snapped at him as he passed, a miniature tree no bigger than a marble, and a perfect red rose that Yasmin warned him was the most dangerous thing in the entire nursery.

Alex supposed that he should have been scared, but mostly he was just excited. He couldn't help it. Creepy plants were *awesome.*

At last, Yasmin stopped walking.

"This is it," she said.

Alex followed her gaze to a tall trellis that had been erected on the opposite side of the tables. Vines twisted up, over, and between the diamond-shaped spaces, their colors bright against the darkness. Some were spiky. Others had thorns. One yellow vine hung lower than the rest, as though weighted down. Along its bottom dangled dozens of tiny sacs about the size of golf balls. Alex caught a whiff of something foul.

"That the vine?" he asked, holding his nose.

"Yeah," Yasmin said. "It's gotten worse. We have to hurry."

"You have something we can cut it down with?"

Yasmin scoffed.

"If it was that easy I would have done it myself," she said. "Look. You see this?" She leaned over the tabletop and pointed to one of the sacs hanging from the underside of the vine. "It's a dangler. They grow on sick plants—the magic kind, at least. Like an infection. This poor vine's got them everywhere now."

Alex leaned over the edge of the table for a closer look. The thin skin of the sac was pulled taut over a black shape, like a chrysalis.

"What's inside?" he asked.

"Could be anything," Yasmin said. "I've only seen two danglers actually open. The first one was just a regular old spider. The second one . . ." She fiddled with her cap. "I don't like to talk about the second one. Luckily, we got it right away."

"We?" Alex asked, surprised. "Natacha actually helped?"

Yasmin gave him a curt nod and continued. She seemed

eager to change the topic as quickly as possible.

"Right now the thing inside this dangler is just chilling," she said, "sucking up plant juice. We cut down the vine, though, and it's like taking a bottle away from a baby. It'll wake up—they'll *all* wake up."

Alex jumped in surprise as the sac in front of him suddenly twitched, causing a chain reaction that continued all the way down the vine, like a string of lights caught in the wind.

"If we can't cut down the vine," he said, "then what do we do?"

"Remove each and every dangler," Yasmin said. "One at a time. If we're careful enough, whatever's growing inside the dangler won't realize that it's been cut off from its food, at least for the first minute or two. That's more than enough time to kill it."

Alex examined the sac in front of him. It dangled slightly from the vine on a purplish strand, like a fruit on its stem. If you managed to twist it just the right way, it looked like it would come off. Still, he couldn't imagine touching the fragile-looking skin without the entire thing bursting in his hand.

"If the dangler breaks . . ." he started.

". . . then the thing inside wakes up instantly," Yasmin said. "In your hands. Not a good thing."

"*My* hands?" Alex asked.

"Don't worry," Yasmin said. "I'll take care of the hard part. You just have to—here, I'll show you."

She handed him a pair of cacti that glowed like phosphorescent coral and then took two of her own. Alex followed her the lengths of three tables until they reached a tiny metal door on the floor. Yasmin placed the cacti around the door like work lights and then lifted it by a curved handle, revealing a hole filled with swirling darkness.

"I'll hand you the dangler," Yasmin said. "You throw it into the void here."

"The void?"

"It's magic," Yasmin said. "There's a few of them in the nursery—the one closest to the door is where I take the trash out every day. Basically, this is the world's greatest garbage chute. You drop something down there, it's gone forever. So, you know, don't stick your hand in."

"I don't think you have to worry about that," Alex said, taking a cautious step back from the hole.

They returned to the beginning of the vine. Lenore was waiting for them. The cat had found a good spot and settled in, confident that something was going to go terribly wrong and wanting to have the best view possible when it happened.

"Stay put," Yasmin told Alex. "I'll twist a dangler off and hand it to you."

"How do I make sure the sac doesn't break?" Alex asked, wishing he had found better gloves.

"Be *gentle,*" Yasmin said. "Like when someone blows bubbles and you catch one on the tip of your finger."

"They always pop when I do that."

"Okay," she said. "Not encouraging. But that's cool. How about this? Hold your hands together, like cupping water. Only the water might eat you if you drop it."

Alex did as she asked. His hands only trembled a little.

"Perfect," Yasmin said, though she didn't look very confident. "We better get started. Try to go as fast as possible. But not *too* fast. Make sure you don't trip. And maybe don't breathe too much. Also, the danglers sometimes move. So be ready for that."

"Anything else?" Alex asked between gritted teeth.

"Nope, that about covers it."

Yasmin climbed onto the rickety table. It wobbled beneath her weight.

"Shouldn't you be wearing gloves too?" Alex asked.

"Need my fingers free," she said. "This takes a delicate touch."

Yasmin reached up and pinched the spot where the sac joined the vine between her thumb and index fingers, then she twisted gently. The sac resisted at first but finally came free, sliding into Yasmin's palm like an egg yolk. She rushed it to Alex's waiting hands. Even through the thick gloves he could feel the heat of the dangler, warm with life. He carried it as quickly as he could to the hole in the floor. Just as he was about to open his hands, Alex felt the small shape inside the amber fluid twitch suddenly, as though it had just woken up.

He dropped it. The darkness swirled faster for just a moment, as though swallowing, and then the dangler was gone.

"See," Yasmin said with a crooked smile. "Easy."

The children shared a look. There was something different between them now, a link that hadn't been there before. For the first time, they were acting as a team.

They moved on to the next one.

Hours ticked by to the steady rhythm of work. Twist, pull, walk, drop. Twist, pull, walk, drop. The danglers came in all shapes and sizes. Most were insectoid in nature, but Alex occasionally glimpsed fur and teeth through the thin sacs. Every so often a dangler shifted in his hands—usually at the last moment, as if sensing what was coming. After nearly losing his hold on one, Alex began to cup them between his hands, like trapping a firefly. He even did this with the danglers that were little more than squishy ooze, though he suspected that these ones hadn't grown correctly and would never wake up at all.

Into the void they went.

By midafternoon, two-thirds of the vine had been cleared. With their goal now in sight, Yasmin grew even more focused. Alex's energy, on the other hand, had begun to flag. His stomach grumbled, and his hands itched like crazy from the gloves. Nevertheless, he refused to suggest a break. He wanted to prove to Yasmin that she could rely on him.

We need to work together, he thought. *Share what we know. That's our best chance of getting out of here.*

As they neared the end of their task, however, he wondered if he was kidding himself. *Is helping Yasmin today going to actually change anything?* She hadn't said a word to him in hours. *What happens if things go back to the way they were after this? What if she refuses to talk to me?*

He couldn't let that happen. This might be his only chance to convince her that they were on the same side.

I should tell her about Unicorn Girl, he thought. *I just have to make sure that Lenore doesn't overhear us. If Natacha finds out what I know, she might kick me out of the library. Or worse.*

He glanced over at the cat. For the first hour she had tracked their every move. When it became clear that nothing interesting was going to happen, however, she placed her head on her paws and closed her eyes. Every so often she would hiss in her sleep and flicker in and out of visibility.

"Yasmin," Alex whispered as she walked along the tabletop, searching for the next dangler. "Can we talk?"

She gave him an annoyed look, anxious to get the work done.

"You need a break?" she asked. "Because Natacha's going to be back soon. We should push on."

"That's not it," Alex said.

"Then what?"

He was just about to tell her when he took another sidelong glance at Lenore. She wasn't there anymore. He heard the tiniest creak of the table to his right, saw a pile of soil flatten as though pressed down by an invisible body.

She's listening, Alex thought. *She probably wasn't ever asleep at all. That was just a trick.*

Yasmin lifted her Mets cap and wiped the sweat from her forehead.

"You ever been to Citi Field?" Alex asked awkwardly. He knew he couldn't talk about Unicorn Girl with Lenore around, and baseball had been the first topic that popped into his head. Yasmin gave him a strange look and then turned her attention to the sac dangling before her. Alex figured that was the end of it, that she would ignore this question just like every other question he had ever asked her about life before the apartment. After a few moments, however, she answered. Maybe she sensed, like Alex, that the silence needed to be filled in order to keep them sharp.

Or maybe she's finally starting to trust me.

"We go on my birthday every year," Yasmin said. "Left-field bleachers. It's sort of a tradition."

"Cool," Alex said. "We've been, too."

"You're a Mets fan?" Yasmin asked, with an actual glimmer of excitement.

"Not really."

"You like the *Yankees*?" she asked.

Judging from the look on her face, Yasmin found this prospect even more disgusting than the danglers.

"Neither one," Alex replied. "My brother's the sports fan. He's this big jock. His room, you walk in and it's nothing but shiny trophies, like a dragon's hoard. An athletic dragon. John's pretty much a slob, except for his trophies. Those he keeps spotless. He has this special cleaning kit my mom got him when his football team won the championship."

Yasmin nodded, half listening while she positioned herself to twist off the next dangler. "You like any sports at all?" she asked.

"Not really," Alex said. "John's always trying to get me to watch more football. He says it's good for me, like a vitamin or something. And then when my attention wanders, because watching people go up and down a field a few feet at a time is really boring, he gets ticked off. 'What's *wrong* with you? Why can't you just like sports like a normal kid?'"

"Your brother sounds like a jerk," Yasmin said, grimacing. She was growing frustrated with the dangler. It wasn't twisting off as easily as the others.

"John isn't all bad," Alex said, suddenly feeling disloyal to his brother by speaking ill of him. "Sometimes he watches old *Twilight Zone* episodes with me. And one time when this kid was being mean to me at school . . ." Alex trailed off, noticing that he had lost Yasmin's attention. "How about you?" he asked. "You have any brothers or sisters?"

Yasmin opened her mouth, about to answer, and then a startled look crossed her face. She glared at Alex with renewed mistrust.

"My family is none of your business," she snapped. "How many times do I have to tell you? We're not friends."

Yasmin turned her back toward Alex with a definitive spin of her heel. Apparently their conversation was over.

It took a lot to make Alex angry, but he felt it bubbling up inside of him now. He was tired and hungry and suddenly feeling foolish for helping this girl in the first place.

"What is your *problem*?" he asked.

"Right now?" Yasmin replied, tugging cautiously on the vine. "This dangler. It's stuck."

"I mean your problem with me."

Yasmin sighed and slowly twisted the dangler in a clockwise motion.

"I don't have a problem with you, Alex."

"Yeah you do," he said. It was nice to let loose, stoke his anger into flames. "You have from the start! I don't get it. We're on the same team!"

"This from the boy who hates sports."

"You know what I mean. We're both prisoners."

"Prisoners?" Yasmin asked with a mocking half smile. "Last time I checked, you spend your days in a comfy library making up stories. Poor thing."

"I'm still trapped here. Like you." His voice softened, the anger having run its course. "You can trust me, Yasmin. I know exactly what you're going through."

"No you do *not*!" Yasmin screeched, her eyes suddenly filling with tears. "You think just because you've been here a week you have any *idea* what it's been like for me? You have no clue. It's all been so easy for you. In fact, you're probably having a blast, like you're the star in one of those stories you write. Only you've never seen Natacha truly lose it, like I have. You've never seen the horror in your friends' eyes as the magic starts to do its work and—"

As Yasmin talked, her attempt to detach the stubborn sac from the vine grew increasingly violent, until she was twisting it from side to side with reckless abandon. Now it finally came free—and immediately slipped out of her fingers, hitting the table with a solid *plop*.

"No!" Yasmin exclaimed.

Two red pincers burst through the outer layer of the sac and dug into the wood, gaining purchase and dragging the rest of the body to freedom. Alex watched in disgust and fascination as dozens of bristly legs shook off the rest of the sac like an unwanted sleeping bag. *It's a centipede,* Alex thought. Except it was more than that, of course. Centipedes didn't have legs that hummed and vibrated like the blades of an electric razor. Nor did they have a periscopic eye dangling from a stalk in the center of their head.

Yasmin brought her foot down, but the creature was too fast.

It skittered along the tabletop, squeezing between pots and along leaves, its body undulating like a snake. As it moved, its vibrating legs spit sawdust into the air and left a long, shallow gouge in the tabletop. It passed over a fallen leaf and shredded it to nothing.

Shredder, Alex thought, naming the creature in his head.

"Get it!" Yasmin exclaimed.

They sprinted toward the back of the nursery, Alex running alongside the table as Yasmin tracked their quarry up top, avoiding the other plants as best she could. When the shredder came close enough to the edge Alex slammed his gloved fist down. He lifted his hand, hoping to see bug guts smeared across the table.

Nothing.

"Where'd it go?" Yasmin asked.

Alex shook his head. He had no idea.

They both listened closely for any possible sound. Even Lenore joined them: ears perked, tiny monkey fingers protruding from her paws. *Ready for action,* Alex thought, with an unexpected feeling of affection for his foe.

Finally, he heard a humming sound above him. Alex looked up just as a many-legged shadow skittered across the underside of the black lights, dusting the plants below with flecks of glass.

"There!" Alex exclaimed, pointing up.

It was too high for the children to reach, even standing on the tabletop. Not too high for Lenore, though. The cat hissed and leaped onto the trellis, clinging to it with her tiny fingers, and climbed upward. She wasn't an expert climber by any means. Slowly but surely, however, she made her way closer to the light fixture hanging from the ceiling.

"Not that I'm complaining," Alex said, "but why is Lenore helping us?"

"She's not," Yasmin said. "She's protecting Natacha's plants."

"Works for me."

They followed the shredder, trying to keep it in sight as it cut a yellow wire with its sharp legs. Electricity sparked in the air. The black lights flickered and then went out altogether. Without them, the plants instantly stopped glowing.

The children were plunged into darkness.

Alex had never been afraid of the dark, but he had also never been in a magical nursery filled with scary plants and a razor-legged centipede before. That changed things. He ran to the nearest source of light, Yasmin by his side. The shredder followed them, dancing across the suspended metal hoods and finding the next yellow wire in no time at all. It was a quick learner.

Another row of black lights went out, birthing a second pocket of darkness.

They moved deeper into the nursery, away from the exit.

"We're going the wrong way," Alex said.

"It's okay," replied Yasmin. "We can still fix this."

"Yasmin—"

"If we don't, Natacha is going to be furious! That might be okay for you, *storyteller*, but not for me. I'm just the girl who waters the plants. I can be replaced!"

The suspended black lights creaked in protest as Lenore leaped onto them, landing gracefully on all four paws and immediately vanishing before their eyes. Alex could still track her progress, however; the lights creaked beneath her weight as the invisible cat stalked her prey. Lenore moved fast for her size. There was no way the centipede was going to make the next wire before twenty pounds of invisible cat caught her.

"Get ready," Alex said. "If Lenore knocks it down, we can't let it get away this time."

They heard a quiet hiss, as though Lenore was getting ready to pounce. Before she could, however, the centipede abruptly changed directions and leaped back onto the trellis, landing on the sick vine. *What's it doing?* Alex wondered, noticing that it was running on the underside of the vine and not along the top.

The first dangler fell, cut loose by those tiny vibrating legs. And then the second. The third.

It's cutting them all free, Alex realized with horror.

Yasmin hopped on the table in one fluid motion, stepping on the first dangler before the sac even opened. By the time she got to the second one, two antennae had poked through the skin, their ends like prickly balls. It met a similar end beneath her sneaker. The third one managed to escape its sac entirely. Alex caught a glimpse of far too many eyes before slamming a potted plant on top of it.

The shredder had already vanished into the darkness. The vine shook, and Alex heard tiny thumps as dangler after dangler fell to the table. Listening closely, he heard other sounds as well.

Scratching. Clicking. Slithering.

Lenore, having finished a quick descent down the trellis, approached the sounds. Her back was arched. The black lights augmented her luminous green eyes.

"Lenore," Alex said. "Don't. There're too many. You'll get hurt."

She looked at him askance, as though the concern in his voice had surprised her, and vanished. In the darkness, they heard a loud yowl as Lenore attacked. More sounds. Hissing. A buzzing noise, like a flying insect. A pot shattering.

Lenore screeched in pain.

Alex knew he shouldn't feel bad. The cat was his enemy, not his friend. But whether it was intentional or not, she was helping them right now. *I can't just let her die.* He took a step toward the darkness, but Yasmin grabbed his arm and shook her head.

"We need to help her," Alex said.

"Lenore can take care of herself," Yasmin said. "You were right before. We should get out of here while we still can."

The trellis shook as something crashed into it. Lenore hissed, and a chorus of foes replied in challenge: sharp chirps and angry chitters and high-pitched squeals. *So many,* Alex thought. Lenore started to hiss a second time, but then there was a snapping sound like a whip smacking concrete, followed by a large thump as something hit the ground.

"Lenore?" Alex asked.

He heard a sizzle of electricity, followed by a blinding flash.

The lights went out. This time, it was all of them.

II

THE KIND OF SHADOWS WITH TEETH

Alex was tempted to sprint full speed toward the exit. The trouble with that was if he tripped or banged into a table, he might lose all sense of direction and start heading the wrong way. Right now, he knew that if he kept walking in a straight line, he would eventually reach the entrance to the apartment. He couldn't risk straying from that.

"Slow and steady," Yasmin whispered, apparently coming to the same conclusion. "Stay together."

Her voice was a comfort in the pitch-black of the nursery. What wasn't comforting were the other sounds: the crunch of leaves torn between incisors, the grinding of tiny teeth against bark. The creatures were doing what all newborns did: eat. It seemed to be keeping them distracted for now, which was good, but Alex was afraid that if they heard two juicy children sneaking by, their appetites might take a quick turn toward the nonvegetarian.

One step at a time, Alex thought, trying to move as quietly as possible. *You'll be there before you—*

He knocked into Yasmin. Something rattled in the dark, taking notice.

"Why'd you stop?" Alex whispered.

"I kicked something," she said. "I think it's Lenore."

Alex bent down, lowering his hand into the darkness. He felt warm, soft fur. *She seems to be breathing okay,* Alex thought, feeling the rising and falling of her rib cage. *But why isn't she moving?* He slid his hand over Lenore's stomach and winced. There was something wet and sticky beneath his fingertips.

Blood.

"She's hurt," he said.

"She'll be fine."

"We have to help her."

"We have more important things to worry about than Natacha's little snitch."

Alex understood where Yasmin was coming from, but he couldn't just leave Lenore behind. Who knew what the other creatures might do to her? He slipped his hands beneath the cat and cradled her to his chest.

"I'll carry her," Alex said.

"Fine," muttered Yasmin.

Boy and girl and cat navigated the darkness.

Alex's ears grew attuned to the slightest sound, but for the most part the dangler-born left them alone. There were a few exceptions. The worst of these was when Alex felt something crawling along the nape of his neck but couldn't do anything about it because he was carrying Lenore. Luckily, Yasmin managed to slap it away just before it scuttled down his back.

After a while, the sounds faded to silence.

"I don't think they're following us anymore," Alex said. "They must be busy eating all the plants."

"Or the other way around," Yasmin said. "A lot of these plants are carnivorous. How's the cat?"

"Heavy. But still breathing."

"I guess it could have been worse," Yasmin said. "At least those things are all trapped in the nursery. If they had gotten into Natacha's precious apartment, then we *really* would have been in trouble."

Alex froze in place. Yasmin took a few steps forward and then stopped as well.

"Alex?" she asked. "I don't hear your footsteps."

"About the closet door," he said. "I don't think it's going to stop them."

"Sure it will," Yasmin said. "You afraid the insects will crawl right under? Don't worry. It doesn't work that way.

When you close the door it seals magically. Nothing can get through."

There was a long silence.

"You *did* close the door, right?" Yasmin asked.

"Mostly," Alex said. "It's just, it was really dark, so I left the door open the tiniest bit to let a little light in. . . ."

Yasmin immediately broke into a run. Alex did the same, though he had no chance of keeping up, especially with a giant cat weighing him down. The slap of Yasmin's sneakers grew distant in the dark.

A few minutes later, he entered the apartment.

It was infested.

Alex's first thought was of a city street at rush hour, except instead of commuters and cars the floor was trafficked by orange roaches and tarantulas and tiny rodents with barbed tails. And not just the floor, either. A gray blur scuttled along an upper bookshelf, knocking magical treasures to the floor. Rubbery strands dangled from the ceiling like jellyfish tentacles. A lizard poked its flat, coin-shaped head out of a torn sofa cushion like a swimmer coming up for air.

That's why the nursery got so quiet, Alex thought. *They all came here.*

Glass shattered in the kitchen. This was quickly followed by a thunderous crash from deeper inside the apartment. Alex suspected that a dresser in one of the bedrooms had fallen over.

"They're everywhere!" Yasmin exclaimed, swatting at a brown bee that had landed on the brim of her cap. "What do we do?"

Alex felt Lenore move in his arms and placed her gently on the floor. She took in the situation, groggy but aware. Her right side was matted with blood, but that didn't stop her from snatching a green worm between her fingers and pulling it apart.

"We might be outnumbered," Alex said. "But we're a lot bigger than they are."

"You focus on the floor," Yasmin said. "I'll swat."

Like one of those city-destroying monsters in the old Japanese movies he loved, Alex stomped across the living room floor, trying to crush anything that moved. Meanwhile, Yasmin grabbed a frying pan from the kitchen and used it on dangler-born squirming along walls or scuttling across countertops.

For a few minutes, they seemed to be making some headway.

Then their prey began to fight back.

Alex heard a loud smack as Yasmin swatted a yellow mosquito on her neck. At almost the same moment, he felt a sharp pain in his ankle. He kicked his foot and a furry lump sailed across the room. Before he could see where it went, something landed on his lower back and immediately began to climb higher, claws tearing through his shirt and into his skin.

"Get it off of me!" he screamed.

"Turn around!" exclaimed Yasmin.

Alex spun in place and felt her hand sweep across his back. A black lizard with eight legs landed on the floor and quickly vanished behind the couch.

"Thanks," Alex said, while backing warily away from the wall. A swarm of dangler-born were congregating there, organizing an attack. "Let's get to the library. I left the door locked, so there's no way they could have gotten inside. Magical seal, right?"

"That's not going to work," Yasmin said. "Look behind you."

Alex turned. Silver webs now covered the two archways leading out of the living room. He picked up a wand that had been knocked from the bookshelf and poked a single strand. It was as solid as steel wire.

No way we're getting past that, Alex thought. *We're trapped.*

The horde of dangler-born crawled down the wall and crossed to the center of the room. Their hisses and rattles took on an almost jubilant tone as they closed in on their prey.

"Any ideas?" Yasmin asked.

"There are like a hundred magical objects in this room," Alex said, raising the wand in his hand. "There must be something we can use."

"I'm not a witch," Yasmin said. "And you're not a wizard."

"Maybe they work for anyone," Alex said, pointing the wand in the direction of the approaching creatures. "Kaboom! Flameo! Freezit!"

Other than making him feel exceedingly foolish, the wand didn't do a thing.

The dangler-born continued their steady approach. Alex pressed his back against the bookshelf. He felt something crawl up his left leg, land on his cheek, in his hair . . .

"WHAT'S GOING ON HERE?"

Natacha stood at the front door, hands on hips, eyes wide with fury. The dangler-born leaped off Alex's body, searching for safety.

"My apartment!" she screeched, taking in the wreckage around her. "What have you done to my beautiful apartment?"

Natacha flicked her two hands outward and the dangler-born vanished in tiny puffs of smoke. She crossed the room, ignoring the children for now, and snapped her fingers. The silver webs blocking the archways shriveled into dust. With her path now cleared, Natacha continued into the other rooms. Alex heard more *puffs* as the remaining intruders were exterminated.

A few moments later, Natacha returned to the living room and sat on her favorite chair, too livid to speak. Alex thought about trying to explain, but he was afraid that if he broke the silence it would be the last thing he ever did. Natacha was a coiled snake looking for a reason to strike.

"I can explain—" Yasmin started.

"No need," Natacha replied, her eyes like chipped ice. "I know what happened. You did something stupid. It brought these vermin into being. They wrecked my apartment. What more do I need to know?"

Lenore limped over and took a seat by her master's side. There were new wounds all over her body, including a particularly nasty gash just beneath her eye.

Natacha waggled her fingers and Lenore's tail solidified into a long block of stone.

"How could you let this happen?" Natacha snapped. Lenore struggled to flee, her new tail dragging against the floor. "You were supposed to be watching them! This is your fault!"

The witch opened her hand and a tiny fireball shot at Lenore. It seared the back of her fur, leaving a black streak against the orange.

Lenore yowled in pain.

"Stop hurting her!" Yasmin exclaimed. "She tried to help!"

"Who gave you permission to speak?" Natacha asked, nostrils flaring.

"Sorry."

"Never had much use for that word," Natacha said. "It ain't magic. It don't undo what you've done. It's just a word." She closed her fists and stretched her fingers like a pianist preparing for a performance. "It's too bad. You were a good little worker while it lasted. You make some mean mashed potatoes, too. Fluffy with just a bit of kick to it. I'll miss those potatoes, I really will." She shrugged. "Oh well. I'm sure your replacement will come knocking at my door any day now. Someone always does."

Natacha raised her hands into the air. When nothing happened, she grimaced and closed her eyes in deep concentration. A bead of sweat ran down her temple.

"Come on," she muttered, like a driver trying to start a car past its prime. "Come on!"

Alex had never seen Natacha struggle to cast a spell before. *It must be especially powerful.* He turned toward Yasmin. Her eyes were terrified, but she showed no inclination to run. Where could she go? There was no escape from the apartment, no use trying to fight. Alex wished there was something he could do to help, but he knew it was pointless. He would only make things worse on himself.

I'm safe, he thought. *It's like Yasmin said—for one reason or another, Natacha needs my stories. She won't hurt me.*

He was ashamed by the relief this thought brought him. *Coward,* he thought. *You're only worried about yourself.* He turned away, unable to look at Yasmin any longer. He felt like he had betrayed her. *Maybe Natacha won't be able to get the spell to work,* Alex thought, but then there was a loud *whoosh,* like the flames finally coming to life in a stubborn old furnace, and the witch's hand began to glow with an eerie blue light.

"Finally," Natacha said, smiling with satisfaction.

She stretched her hands toward Yasmin. Lightning danced between her fingertips, the magic anxious to be unleashed. Yasmin's eyes widened, and she muttered something that might have been a name. Alex felt her fear as though it were his own. They might not have been friends, but there was still a link between them, a shared experience that no one else could ever understand.

I can't let this happen, he thought.

Alex scraped together as much bravery as he could and stepped in front of Yasmin.

"It wasn't her fault," he said. His voice trembled. "It was mine."

"Move, storyteller," Natacha snarled.

"I couldn't think of a new idea for a story," Alex said, his mind assembling the details on the fly. "And so I begged

Yasmin to take me down to the nursery. I thought, creepy plants, maybe I can think of something cool. She made me promise not to touch anything, only when she wasn't looking I got curious and fed one of the vines. Guess I fed it the wrong thing, because the next thing I know it had all these sacs hanging from it."

Alex caught a glimpse of Yasmin's flabbergasted expression. She couldn't believe that he was taking the blame for her.

"*You* did this?" Natacha asked, wincing as a fresh volley of lightning snapped between her fingers. Her hands had begun to shake violently. She balled them into fists, trying to keep the magic in check. "You're more trouble than you're worth, storyteller."

Alex realized that he had made a horrible mistake. The fact that he wrote scary stories might have helped him if Natacha was thinking logically, but right now she was barely thinking at all. She just wanted to punish someone.

The witch stretched her hands toward him. He closed his eyes.

"No, no, no," she commanded. "You have to open your eyes or you'll ruin the final—"

The apartment began to quake.

"No!" Natacha exclaimed. "Not now!"

The distraction caused the witch to lose her hold on the spell. Blue fire shot from her hands and struck the wall with an anticlimactic puff of smoke. *The spell only works on people,* Alex thought, wondering what it would have done to him.

"Story!" Natacha exclaimed, grasping him by the shirt and drawing him close. "Now!"

Alex did as he was told without hesitation; he had tested his luck enough for today. As the apartment continued to rumble, he ran to the library, snagged the nightbook on the desk, and hustled back. In his absence a large crack had appeared on the living room wall. A sickly sweet smell, like cotton candy left in the car on a hot summer's day, filled the room.

"What is that?" Alex asked, holding his nose.

"It doesn't matter," Natacha said. "Just read your story. And for your sake, it better be a good one."

THE PLAYGROUND

Foster Playground was where all the dead kids played. You could hear them at night, giggling and whispering. Even when there was no wind, swings arced high into the sky and the seesaw squeaked up and down.

Todd knew to stay away. He had heard stories about the bad things that happened there. But when his best friend, Jenny, died, his heart shattered into a thousand pieces and all he could think about was how badly he wanted to see her again.

The night after her funeral, he snuck out of his house and went to the playground.

It was a warm summer evening, but as soon as Todd stepped onto the wood chips he began to shiver. The air was different here. Not just colder, but with a metallic taste, like biting down on an old coin. It wasn't air meant for living people.

I don't belong here, Todd thought.

He almost left. But then he remembered Jenny, and how lonely she must feel, and willed his feet across the wood chips. Crunch. Crunch. Crunch. Soon Todd stood before the tall wooden tower at the center of the playground. Two enclosed slides coiled from its top. One was red and one was green, but they both looked the same in the dark.

Suddenly there was a loud thump at the top of the tower, and the slide rattled and shook beneath the weight of a passenger. Seconds later, a boy about Todd's age shot out of the hole in the bottom. His skin was pale, and he wore clothes that Todd had seen only in black-and-white movies.

The pale boy examined Todd from head to toe. When he seemed satisfied, he placed two fingers in his mouth and whistled loudly. New faces peeked down at them from the top of the tower. Soon children were pouring from the slides. Girls and boys, toddlers and teenagers. Some wore old clothes, though none as old as the pale boy's. Others wore clothes like Todd's. Everyone seemed happy to see him. They jostled for position, trying to get as close to Todd as possible, as though he were a fire by which they could warm their hands.

No one spoke. Their smiles were bright and wide.

Todd asked if Jenny was there, but the children just laughed and ushered him from one piece of playground equipment to the next. They gave him no time to think. Giggles chased him to the top of the rock wall. Cold hands pushed him on the swings.

They played for hours.

From the top of the tower, the pale boy watched it all. At one point, Todd thought he saw a second figure up there as well, a girl. She kept trying to reach the slides, but the pale boy blocked her path.

In time, Todd found himself laughing along with the other children. It was hard to remember why he had been so scared to come here. Foster Playground was a nice place. It was where he belonged. He only wished he were warmer. His body felt encased in ice, and it was becoming harder and harder to breathe. He looked up at the pale boy, wondering if he knew what was going on, but the boy wasn't looking in his direction anymore. He was looking at the sky, where threads of morning sunlight were just beginning to appear.

The boy's face curled into a wicked smile. In a flash, Todd remembered the stories he had heard about this place. Finally, he understood.

If I'm still here in the morning, I'll be here forever.

He spun around, trying to escape, but the children grabbed him and pulled him back. They were no longer smiling. Todd tried to shout for help, but all that came out were plumes of cold air. The children dragged him backward, giggling, making a game of it now. Todd's feet left shallow trails in the wood chips.

Above him, he could see the sun starting to rise. Morning was just a few minutes away.

He heard the sound of someone coming down the slide and watched the opening, expecting to see the pale boy, his mocking grin. Except it wasn't the pale boy. It was Jenny. She shoved the children away and helped Todd to his feet.

Go! she mouthed. *Go! Go!*

Todd ran as fast as he could, racing the children to the edge of the playground. He felt tiny hands claw at the back of his shirt . . . and then he leaped onto the safety of grass.

When he turned around, the children were already walking with slumped shoulders back toward the wooden tower. Only Jenny remained looking in his direction.

"Thank you," Todd said, tears filling his eyes. "And good-bye."

She smiled sadly and vanished in the morning light.

As Alex reached the end of the story, the apartment gave one final shudder—knocking a jade talisman off its pedestal—and stopped rumbling completely. Yasmin sighed with relief. Alex's feelings were more complicated. He was glad that the apartment hadn't crumbled into dust, but unnerved by the power his stories held over such an evil place. *Does that prove there's something wrong with me?* he wondered. Alex's thoughts drifted to the story he refused to tell Natacha, the real reason he had decided to toss his nightbooks in the furnace. He had been in math when the phone rang. . . .

Natacha grabbed his arm, breaking his train of thought.

"Seriously?" she asked. "That's the end of the story?"

The murderous fury had left her eyes, but she didn't exactly look happy, either.

"Was it bad?" Alex asked, warmth spreading over his face.

"No," Natacha said. "That's the point. It's not bad at all. The boy gets away, safe and sound."

"Sometimes that happens."

"Not in my experience."

The story wasn't dark enough for her, Alex thought. There were creepy dead kids, which was always good, but at its heart "The Playground" was more about friendship than ghosts. Alex had written it after his best friend moved to New Jersey.

"How about this instead?" Natacha suggested. "The ghosts follow the boy home and kill him in his sleep. *Much* better."

"The ghosts can't leave the playground."

"That isn't even a thing!" the witch insisted. "Ghosts haunt houses and castles and hotels—maybe the occasional school. I've never heard of a ghost haunting a playground, and I'm a witch, which makes me an—"

"Jenny helps Todd escape," Alex said. His cheeks were still red, but now it was from stubbornness, not embarrassment. "That's what happens. She's a true friend even after her death."

"You mean it's a . . . *happy ending*?" Natacha asked, mortified.

Alex shrugged his shoulders.

"It's not exactly happy," he said. "Jenny is still dead, and she's going to be trapped in that playground for eternity. Does that make you feel better?"

"A little," Natacha admitted. "But what I think isn't important. Happy endings can be dangerous things. You soothed the apartment this time, but your story just as easily could have—"

"I liked it," Yasmin said.

Natacha and Alex turned in surprise. It was the first time that Yasmin had spoken during their story sessions.

"No one asked *you*," snarled Natacha. She shook her

head at the debris covering the living room floor. "Clean this place up, storyteller. Girl—attend to the nursery. Make sure you repot any plants that can still be saved. I have some new orders coming in, and I don't want to be short on ingredients. When I wake up tomorrow, I expect this place to be spotless."

Alex and Yasmin exchanged a look of relief. Considering the alternative, staying up all night cleaning seemed like a small punishment indeed. They immediately set to work on their assigned tasks. Yasmin smiled at Alex and waved good-bye before entering the nursery. He waved back. Meanwhile, Natacha shuffled across the floor, her gait like that of an old woman, and paused before the wall with the big crack. She raised a hand, as though to cast some sort of spell, and then thought better of it and continued toward her bedroom at the end of the hall. Natacha's body blocked his view of the keyhole, but the telltale scratching of a bonekey left little doubt that she was going into her secret room. Whenever Natacha had done this in the past, she always glanced over her shoulder first to make sure that no one was watching. If Yasmin or Alex happened to be in the nearby vicinity, she would send them away before opening the door.

Tonight, however, Natacha's exhaustion had gotten the better of her. Without so much as a glance over her shoulder, she carelessly opened the door wide and stepped across the threshold. For just a moment, Alex was able to see past her.

Night sky. Pine trees. Forest floor.

Natacha closed the door.

It's not a room, Alex thought, his heart fluttering with excitement. *It's an exit! We can use it to escape!*

All they needed was the witch's key.

By the time Alex finally crawled beneath the blankets, his entire body ached. Still, he was in a good mood. There were some stains that would require a second scrubbing in the morning, but other than that the apartment had been restored to its predangler state.

He closed his eyes and thought about Natacha's keys. *She never puts them down. Ever. So how do I get ahold of them?* His mind cycled through possible ideas, looking for one that fit. It was like trying to figure out what should happen next when he was writing a story.

Could I pickpocket her?

Not without getting caught.

What about when she sleeps?

Natacha locked her bedroom door at night, so that wouldn't work. He'd need a key to steal the key.

Can I use any of the magical artifacts on the shelves?

Alex didn't think so. He had handled many of them while cleaning and felt nothing magical at all. If he were a warlock, then maybe—

Why are you thinking so hard? he heard his older brother interject. *Just hit her over the head with a frying pan and be done with it.*

Alex could see all sorts of problems with that plan, too. What if he missed? What if she didn't lose consciousness? What if Lenore stopped him?

It was too big of a risk.

He wished he could brainstorm ideas with Yasmin. She understood Natacha and the apartment a lot better than him.

But can I trust her?

He didn't know. It was clear that Yasmin had experienced some horrible things. He remembered what she'd said, about seeing the horror in her friends' eyes. *There must have been other prisoners before me,* Alex thought. *That's why she's scared of acting out against Natacha. She's seen firsthand what happens when you don't behave.* If he told her what he was planning, Yasmin might immediately spill the beans rather than risk getting in trouble.

Then again, he thought, *I'm not sure I have a choice. I can't do this on my own.*

He turned on his side, too tired to think about it any longer. Despite his exhaustion, sleep refused to come. He shivered in fear, wondering if Yasmin's friend had once slept in the same bed as him—if not the bottom bunk, then maybe the top one. *What about the mystery girl who wrote in the storybooks? Did she sleep here, too? What if she didn't escape? What if one night—asleep in this very bed—Natacha crept into this room and dragged her out. . . .*

He heard a rustling sound.

Alex sat up in bed, instantly awake.

"Who's there?" he asked.

The noise continued. He crept out of bed, his bare feet icy cold on the wooden floor, and carefully scanned the room. The rustling was coming from the closet. *Natacha must have missed one of the dangler-born*, he thought. Seeing no better weapon available, he picked up one of his sneakers (still sticky with bug guts) and padded across the floor.

Alex gathered his courage and then opened the door quickly, intending to take his visitor by surprise.

The sound stopped.

The closet looked no different than usual. His backpack was tucked into one corner. Above it, clothes and empty hangers hung from a wooden rod.

"What the heck?" Alex asked, mystified.

He lifted his bag, wondering if something might be hiding behind it, and a dark shape scuttled out of a hole torn in the side. With a shriek of surprise, Alex dropped the backpack and kicked the closet door shut, catching the insect just as it was crossing the threshold. There was a crunching noise, like someone squeezing a fistful of potato chips, and the insect stopped moving.

The shredder, Alex thought, recognizing the dozens of sharp, bristly legs. *Must have been hiding in my backpack when Natacha cleaned out the apartment.*

He glanced at the bag, wondering what the shredder had been up to this entire time, and his heart froze. A trail of torn paper spilled from the hole. With trembling hands, Alex knelt down and unzipped the backpack.

"No!" he exclaimed.

He turned the entire bag over, hoping that there was some kind of mistake, that his two nightbooks would fall to the floor and all would be well. They didn't. Instead, shredded paper rained down, collecting in a pile in front of him. He could make out the occasional word—*phantom, bird, coffin*—but mostly it was just incoherent letters.

His stories had been destroyed.

12

YASMIN'S STORY

After discovering the fate of his nightbooks, Alex was too upset to sleep. He couldn't stop thinking about the hours spent writing each story: the shock of discovery when a new character stepped out of the shadows, the frustration when a plot withered and died, the sheer bliss of unearthing a perfect word. The writing had been agonizing at times, but it had also been wonderful.

And now I have nothing to show for it, he thought.

More than anything else, Alex regretted not sharing the stories when he had a chance. He pictured a graveyard with the words *They Died Unread* etched into each tombstone and felt a mixture of guilt and loss. Unfortunately, resurrecting the stories wasn't a possibility. Alex might remember some of the plots and characters, but piecing them back together again would be like reassembling a cracked eggshell. No matter how hard he tried, the stories would never be the same.

There was no time to grieve for what he had lost, however. Without those two nightbooks, Alex no longer had a stockpile of stories from which to draw. His situation had become more perilous than ever.

How many stories do I have left? How many days before Natacha no longer has any use for me?

Alex needed to know.

He sprinted to the library, suddenly convinced that the final nightbook had also been torn to bits, and sighed with relief when he found it safe and sound on the desk. Alex carefully flipped through its pages, taking stock of the stories that he hadn't yet read to Natacha. He found one that would work, and then a second that he had abandoned midway, thinking it a lost cause. Alex read it again. Sometimes he would revisit a draft after a week or two and find that it was a lot better than he thought. Unfortunately, this particular story had not improved—in fact, it was even worse than he remembered. He continued flipping. There were two more stinkers, and then another story near the back of the book that wasn't half bad.

Two stories. That was all he had left.

"Okay," Alex said, pacing back and forth. "No big deal. I just have to start writing again. Plenty of time."

Alex sat in front of the open nightbook and smoothed

down a fresh page. Despite his lack of sleep, he felt energized. He hadn't written anything in over a week, and he was excited to make up for lost time.

This is going to be fun, Alex thought.

He picked up a pencil and started to jot down some ideas.

Three hours later, Alex was sitting in the exact same position. The gears of his mind, which normally spun like a well-oiled engine, felt clogged with molasses. He couldn't come up with a single good idea. The harder he tried, the more difficult it became. He remembered another term that Ms. Coral had written on the board: *WRITER'S BLOCK.* Alex hadn't liked that one nearly as much as *interior logic.*

At last, someone knocked on the door. Alex leaped out of his seat to answer it.

"Good morning," Yasmin said.

She looked different. For one thing, she wasn't wearing her Mets cap. Her long hair, still wet from a recent shower, fell straight down her back. Gone, too, were the work clothes she normally wore, replaced by jeans and a faded gray T-shirt a size too big for her. The difference in Yasmin was more than just her physical appearance, however. She stood straight and proud, with a relaxed confidence that Alex had never seen before. He felt like he was meeting the real girl for the first time.

"Hey," Alex said.

"Hey," replied Yasmin. There was a stone mortar filled with gray paste in her hands. She held it out now like a new neighbor delivering a pie. "I made a poultice from some plants in the nursery. I figure you have a ton of bites and scratches from yesterday. This will help with the pain."

"Thanks," Alex said, taking it. "That was really nice of you."

"If you hadn't taken the blame for what happened yesterday, I wouldn't be standing here right now. It seemed the least I could do."

"It was no big deal," Alex said, fighting a blush and losing. "Any idea what kind of spell she was going to cast on us?"

Yasmin nodded.

"We'll get to that," she said. "Can you take a break for a few minutes? I know you have a lot of questions, and . . . I figure it's time someone told you a story for a change." She nodded toward a nasty gash on his hand. "But get some poultice on that first. It looks pretty bad."

Alex did as she suggested. The pain instantly started to fade.

"Wow," he said, already smearing a substantial amount across a second wound on his forearm. "How'd you learn to make this stuff? I thought Natacha only sold oils."

"This isn't for sale," Yasmin said. "It's for her prisoners.

In case someone gets hurt, she wants them up and about as quickly as possible. There are oils to be made, you know. Or in your case, stories to be written." She took a deep, lingering breath, like a student before a final exam. "You want to sit down before I start? This could take a while."

"Hold on," he said. "I'm dying to hear your whole story, I really am, but first . . ." He raised the mortar. "There's someone who needs your poultice a lot more than I do."

They found Lenore curled up in the corner of the kitchen. Her orange-and-black fur was spotted with blood, but at least her tail looked better. The stone that previously encased it had shattered, littering the floor with pebbles.

Alex knelt down beside her.

"Hey, Lenore," he said softly. "I have medicine. It will make you feel better."

The cat managed to raise her head a few inches off the floor and hiss. It was as fearsome as air leaking from a bicycle tire.

"At least we don't have to worry about getting scratched," Yasmin said with reluctant sympathy. "The poor thing can barely move."

Alex dabbed a bit of poultice on two fingers and lowered it toward a bite mark on Lenore's stomach.

The cat vanished.

"I can't help you if I can't see you," Alex said in a parental tone. When Lenore didn't reappear, he added, "Have it your way," and smeared the poultice in the general vicinity of the bite. At first the cat squirmed feebly, trying to avoid his touch. After just a few seconds, however, she grew suddenly still.

"See," Alex said. "It feels better, doesn't it? Now stop being so stubborn and let me do this the right way."

Lenore turned barely visible, like a light at its dimmest setting.

Fine, her expression seemed to say. *But this is all you get.*

Alex gently spread the poultice over the cat's wounds. Lenore stiffened when he touched some of the nastier spots, but for the most part bore his ministrations without complaint.

"Can you do that and listen to me at the same time?" Yasmin asked. "I've been holding everything inside for so long, and now I feel like I'm going to explode if I wait any longer."

Alex nodded in understanding. He had often felt the same way when sitting down to write a story.

"Maybe we should talk somewhere else," he suggested, looking meaningfully at Lenore. He lowered his voice to a whisper. "She might be out of it, but she's still listening. Anything you say—"

"This is all stuff that Natacha knows anyway," Yasmin said. "Nothing that will get us in trouble."

"Okay."

Yasmin started to take a seat, then changed her mind and paced back and forth across the kitchen floor. As she walked, she tucked her hands beneath her chin and wrung them together.

"My first night in the apartment I cried my eyes out," Yasmin said. "I had no idea what was happening. All I knew was that some woman had tricked me into coming inside and now I was trapped. It wasn't until the next morning that I learned I wasn't alone. There were three others. Eli. Little Hwan. And Claire." She smiled sadly, remembering. "They taught me what I needed to know. Eli was in charge of the cooking. Hwan did the cleaning. I learned how to tend to the plants in the nursery from Claire. She was a year older than me, with this big smile that could light up an entire room. She had been Natacha's prisoner the longest, but she hadn't lost her optimistic attitude. She kept saying that if we stuck together, everything would be all right."

Except they're gone now, Alex thought, *so everything didn't turn out all right.* He sat perfectly still, no longer tending to Lenore, just listening. Part of him was riveted, but another part wanted to cover his ears before Yasmin's tale took its inevitable turn into darkness. For the first time in his life, Alex understood why some people stopped reading a scary story in the middle.

"At night we took turns reading to Natacha from one of the books in the library. All of us except Hwan, that is. He didn't really know how to read yet. After Natacha had gone to sleep we huddled together in Claire's room and tried to come up with an escape plan. Eli, who was kind of a hothead, insisted that if we all charged Natacha at once we could tie her up and then she'd have to let us go. Claire disagreed. She didn't think we stood a chance against Natacha's magic. She said that we just had to be patient and wait for our opportunity. It would come. Hwan didn't say anything at all. Mostly he just clung to Claire. Sometimes he cried and she rocked him to sleep like a baby."

"How about you?" Alex asked.

"I was team Claire, all the way," Yasmin said. "In everything. We only knew each other for a few weeks, but it didn't matter. Living through such a horrible experience pushes you together a lot faster than regular life. She became my sister. Hwan and Eli were my brothers. I'm not saying I was happy. None of us were happy. But at least we had each other."

Silence settled. Alex realized that Yasmin had reached the most difficult part of the story. She wouldn't continue unless he nudged her forward, like a reader turning a page.

"Tell me what happened," he said.

She looked up. Her eyes were wet with memory.

"I don't have to tell you," she said. "I can show you."

Alex left a handful of Froot Loops by Lenore's side and followed Yasmin into the dining room. She stopped in front of the antique china cabinet and studied the porcelain children lining the shelves. Alex followed her gaze. Until this point he hadn't paid much attention to the figurines, but now he noticed that there was something off about their gleeful expressions.

The smiles look forced, he thought. *Like when a photographer takes too long to snap a picture and you have to keep smiling whether you want to or . . .*

Alex shivered as the truth hit him.

"These are the kids who lived here before us," he said, wondering why he hadn't figured it out earlier. "Natacha turned them into . . . little statues."

Yasmin nodded.

"That's Hwan," she said, pointing to a figure of a small Asian boy sitting in a rocking chair. He was holding a stuffed rabbit. "In the end he couldn't keep up with the work like the rest of us. Natacha finally lost her patience. And there—Eli." Yasmin pressed her finger against the glass, inches from a rangy boy with a mop of blond hair. He was smiling like all the others—Alex supposed that was a creepy side effect of the spell—but his eyes were shut tight in one final act of defiance. "He went ahead with his plan and tried to jump Natacha when she least expected it," Yasmin said. "It didn't work."

She knelt down, her eyes level with the bottom shelf of the china cabinet now. Alex identified Claire before Yasmin even pointed to her, a pretty girl drawing water from a well, with eyes that radiated kindness. She looked like someone who would grow up to be a teacher or a nurse.

"In the end it was just the two of us," Yasmin said. "Me and Claire. Until one day there was a knock at the door. That happens sometimes. We get visitors. Grocery delivery. Landlord. Neighbors. Even the police, from time to time."

"Not since I've been here," Alex said.

"I'm sure people have come," Yasmin explained, "only when Natacha's not in the apartment, we can't even hear the knocking—and they can't hear us, either. It's like there's a wall between us and the outside world. But that changes when Natacha's home. Occasionally she has to let people inside. If not, someone might grow suspicious."

Alex wondered if his family had ever knocked on the door to apartment 4E. Maybe he had been standing on the other side of the wall at the time, just a few feet away.

"That day was different than usual," Yasmin continued, "because we were actually expecting a visitor. The pipes in the kitchen sink had been leaking for a week, and there wasn't anything that Natacha's magic could do to fix it—which was a little bit funny—so she had finally called the plumber. Claire and I did as we were told and stayed in the nursery. We could scream and shout all we wanted to down there, but no one would hear a thing in the apartment. While we waited in the dark, Claire took my hands and told me the truth. She had broken the kitchen pipes herself, knowing that a plumber would have to come. There was a note taped to the underside of the sink, explaining everything. It begged whoever found it to send help as quickly as possible."

"That was a good idea," Alex said.

"It was," replied Yasmin. "Only Natacha figured it out somehow, and when she unlocked the door to the nursery, the note was in her hands." Yasmin cleared her throat. "Claire didn't even try to talk her way out of it. She spent her last minutes making sure Natacha knew that I hadn't been involved."

Yasmin looked drained, like someone recovering from a long illness, but not nearly as sad anymore. By sharing her story, she had shed a portion of her grief.

"So now you know," Yasmin said. "That's why I was so mean to you in the beginning. I didn't want to risk getting close to someone else and losing them again. I'm sorry."

She hugged him, and Alex hugged her back. It should have been weird and awkward—she was a girl, after all—but it wasn't that way at all. It felt right.

They were still trapped, but they were no longer alone.

"Can the spell on your friends be reversed?" Alex asked when they had parted. "You know, like in a fairy tale, when the witch dies and everything goes back to the way it was in the end."

"This isn't a story, Alex. Claire had it right the first time. All we can really do is be patient and hope something changes." She peeked into the kitchen to make sure Lenore hadn't moved. "I agree with you about the blue mist," she whispered. "I think it's what keeps the witch young. For all we know, Natacha could be hundreds of years old, maybe thousands. We're just kids. How can we hope to outsmart her?"

Alex stared at the figurines through his ghostly reflection in the glass. He remembered what Natacha had said his second day in the apartment, when she was on the verge of casting the spell that would have added him to her collection: *"Just be a doll and stand still. And whatever you do, don't close your eyes. Like a photograph."*

It gave him an idea.

"Are those the same outfits that your friends were wearing when the spell was cast on them?" he asked.

"Why?"

"Just go with it."

"Um . . . yeah," Yasmin said. "Those hideous smiles are fake—and I doubt that Claire ever got water from a well in her life—but everything else is right on target. Look, you can even see Hwan's little watch. He always wore that thing."

"Good," Alex said, scanning the figurines more carefully now. "That means it should definitely be there."

"What?" Yasmin asked.

"I'll tell you in a second."

He traced his finger along the glass, trying not to rush. *If I'm right,* he thought, *this changes everything.* He searched the figurines once, and then a second time, just to make sure. There was no question about it.

No one was wearing a unicorn pendant.

She promised that she would never take it off, Alex thought with rising excitement. *That means she isn't there! Natacha never turned her into a figurine!*

"There's a way out of this place," he said. "I don't know how yet, but I'm positive it can be done."

"What makes you so sure?"

Alex smiled.

"Because I know someone who escaped," he said.

13

WRITER'S BLOCK

Alex and Yasmin went back to the library and closed the door behind them.

"I have so much to tell you," Alex said.

In his eagerness to finally share everything, Alex inadvertently abandoned all his storytelling skills. He hopped from topic to topic, sometimes in midsentence, and often lost his train of thought. Fortunately, Yasmin asked good questions, forcing him to backtrack when necessary. In the end, she managed to learn everything there was to know about Unicorn Girl, the forest that Alex had glimpsed through the bedroom door, and his sudden shortage of stories.

Gradually, the resigned look in Yasmin's eyes was replaced by a glimmer of hope.

"You really think we can get out of here?" she asked.

"Yes."

"What's the plan?"

The children smiled at one another.

"We need to search the rest of these books," Alex said. "Unicorn Girl might have written about her escape plan. If it worked for her, maybe it will work for us."

"And if she didn't write it down?"

"Then maybe she said something else that can help us," Alex said. "You never know. The more we learn about Natacha, the better."

Yasmin tilted her head upward in order to take in the thousands of books that still needed to be searched.

"You can't do this on your own. Show me where you left off and I'll start looking."

"Don't you have nursery stuff to do?" Alex asked.

"I'll be okay," Yasmin said. "I'll just get up earlier tomorrow and take care of my chores first. Right now finding how this girl got out of here is the second most important thing we've got to do."

"What's the first most—"

Yasmin gave him a playful shove toward the desk.

"You have to write," she said. "This whole plan falls apart if Natacha decides to make a porcelain Alex out of you."

For the rest of the day, he sat at the desk and tried to think of a good idea. Nothing came. Alex knew from experience that forcing an idea to the surface seldom worked; it only scared them away, like screaming at a flock of birds while expecting one to land on your finger. You had to let them come at their own pace. This was all well and good when you were writing stories in your bedroom at night, stories that no one would ever read, but not when your life depended on it.

His frustration grew. Pencil points snapped. Pages were torn.

When Alex's sighs of dismay grew impossible to ignore, Yasmin dropped the stack of books she was searching and stood over him, arms akimbo.

"Okay," she said. "What's the issue?"

"I have complete and total writer's block," Alex said, plunking his head on the desk. "In fact, I think it's fair to say that I'm never going to write another sentence again for the rest of my life."

"Don't be dramatic," Yasmin said. "You're probably just thinking too hard. You remember any of the stories from the notebooks that got torn up?"

"Some of them," he said. "But it doesn't matter. I can't write them all over again."

"Why not?"

"Because I *wrote them already*," Alex said. "If I do it again, they won't be the same."

"Maybe they'll be better."

"You don't understand," Alex said, turning his head away. "Just forget it."

Yasmin kicked his foot.

"You don't have time to be grumpy," she said. "Who cares if they're the same or not? They're just stories."

"They're not *just* stories!" Alex exclaimed. "Some of my favorites were in those nightbooks! Like there was this one I was really proud of about this girl who moves into a new house, and there's this tree in her backyard that promises her it will grant her wish if she hangs up something she truly loves in its branches, and at first the girl is thrilled because she's getting these awesome wishes in exchange for little stuff, like necklaces and toys, only the tree keeps wanting more valuable things, until finally it asks for her baby brother, and the girl knows it's wrong but she's sort of changed with getting all her wishes granted so she goes to the crib one night and—"

"I'm confused," Yasmin interjected.

"Sorry," Alex asked. "I'm bad at summarizing. The plot would make a lot more sense if you could read it, which of course you can't, because—"

"I'm not confused about the story," Yasmin said. "I'm confused about the nightbooks. You seem really bummed that they're gone, but weren't you going to chuck them in the fire anyway? You couldn't have liked those stories *that* much."

The words hit Alex like a cold splash of water. For a few moments he was too astonished to speak.

"You're right," he said. "I was going to destroy all three of them myself. That's what got me into this whole mess in the first place. So now that they're gone, why do I miss them so much?"

"Beats me," Yasmin said. "I never understood why you were getting rid of them in the first place."

Alex thought about telling her what had happened in school that day, after the math teacher got her phone call, but he was afraid it might change her opinion of him. He told her a lesser truth instead.

"I wanted to be someone different," Alex said, "not the weird kid who likes monsters."

"But you *are* weird," she said. "So what? It's cool."

"It's *not* cool," Alex insisted. "Instead of sports trophies like my brother, you know what's on my shelves? Stupid plastic models of vampires and werewolves and mummies. When my family and I go on vacation, I beg them to take me on ghost tours instead of amusement parks." He lowered his voice, as if confessing a great secret. "I have *Walking Dead* pajamas."

"And I can tell you the number of every Mets player all the way back to 2003, even the guys who only had a few at bats," countered Yasmin. "I spent an entire winter break memorizing them. Don't believe me? Xavier Nady, number twenty-two! Willie Collazo, number thirty-six!" She shrugged her shoulders. "We all have our things."

Alex wondered if she might be right. Was writing scary stories any stranger than memorizing random numbers sewn to the backs of uniforms? It made him feel better, thinking about it like that.

Maybe it's not just me who's weird, Alex thought. *Maybe we're all weird in different ways.*

Yasmin leaned over the desk and spun the nightbook in her direction.

"I thought you said you couldn't come up with any ideas," she said. "There's a whole list here."

Alex snatched the book away.

"Don't look," he said. "They're awful."

"You're probably just being too picky," Yasmin said. "Come on—hit me with them."

Alex hesitated. He never shared his ideas before a story was completely finished. On the other hand, nothing else was working, and he was growing desperate. If he didn't think of an idea soon, he'd find himself without a story to tell Natacha in a couple of nights.

He slid the nightbook across the desk. The list was a pitted battlefield of pencil slashes and erasure marks:

STORY IDEAS

- ~~Girl who finds out her parents are monsters~~
- ~~Kids who go to the bathroom during class but never come back~~
- ~~Mailbox that eats people~~
- ~~School locker that leads into another world~~
- ~~Creepy house at Halloween~~
- ~~Kale~~
- ~~Ghost that haunts other ghosts~~
- ~~Nightmarecatcher~~

"Let's see," Yasmin said, running her finger down the page with a thoughtful expression. "How about this one? 'Mailbox that eats people.' I can see that. You reach in for the mail, something bites you. Pretty scary."

"As an idea, maybe," Alex conceded. "But where do I go from there? 'The mailbox ate Bob's hand. Bob got an ax and chopped down the mailbox.' There's not much to it."

"Maybe the mailbox needs to deliver Bob's hand somewhere."

"Eww," Alex said, impressed.

"Let's see what else you have," she said. 'Creepy house at Halloween'?"

"Because that's never been done before."

"You're not being graded on originality, Alex. You just need a story. Here, I'll get you started. 'All the kids were afraid to trick-or-treat at Bob's house, because . . .'"

". . . he had a meat hook instead of a hand, due to a terrible experience with a mailbox."

"Funny," Yasmin said, with just a hint of a smile. "What about this one? 'Ghost that haunts other ghosts'? That's different."

"Same problem with the mailbox one," Alex said. "It sounds good on paper, but there's no way to make it into a story. Why would a ghost haunt another ghost?"

"I don't know," Yasmin said. "Why do they haunt people?"

"Revenge, usually," Alex said. "They could have been murdered. Or someone moved into the house they used to live in and they still think of it as *their* house."

"Sounds like they're just jealous because they're not alive anymore."

"Hmm," Alex said.

He picked up his pencil and added "jealous ghost" to the list. It wasn't enough to start a story, but there was something there, something he could use—he could feel it. Ms. Coral had taught him that good writers didn't necessarily come up with better ideas than other people; they simply recognized the good ones.

"Jealous ghost," Yasmin read, nodding her head in consideration. "That could work."

"Maybe," Alex said. "Let me think about it."

"Do your thing," Yasmin said. "I'll keep searching the books. I have to tell you, though—I'm starting to wonder if this is all a wild-goose chase. Maybe you already found everything this girl has written."

She was wrong.

14

THE MISSING INGREDIENT

Alex woke up early the next morning and trudged back to the library. He hadn't made any headway with his "jealous ghost" story the day before, but his ideas grew best in the soil of sleep and he felt on the verge of a breakthrough.

The story's almost loose, he thought. *I just have to pry it out.*

He sat in his chair and got straight to work.

The first story he wrote was called "Quarters." It was about a dead kid who misses video games and haunts this retro arcade. He gets jealous since all he can do is watch the living kids play, so he messes up their games, making the screens flicker and bug out at inopportune moments. Alex got about two pages into the story and stopped. It wasn't working. He couldn't say exactly why.

It was like a potential friendship that had all the right ingredients but no chemistry.

As Yasmin entered the library and started searching the shelves, Alex flipped to a new page.

In his second story, a recently deceased girl grows envious of the ghost next door, who haunts a much nicer house. Alex got a little further into this one, close to four pages, before giving up. *It's no good!* he thought, slapping the can of pencils off the desk. He removed his glasses and rubbed his eyes with the palms of his hands. After reading to Natacha last night, he was down to his final story. The pressure was making it hard to concentrate.

Yasmin shouted in jubilation.

"I found another entry!" she exclaimed, holding a book aloft. Or, at least, Alex assumed that was what she was holding. Yasmin had climbed past the midway point of the tower and was little more than a small figure in the distance.

"Don't read it!" Alex shouted, cupping his hands to his mouth. "Wait for me!"

"Okay! I'm heading down!"

The stairs shook beneath Yasmin's feet. Alex, too excited to wait, started toward her. They met somewhere in the middle and huddled together on the stairs, their backs pressed against a bookcase.

"She wrote a lot this time," Yasmin said.

"Good," Alex said, out of breath. "The more we know, the better."

Yasmin propped the book, titled *Stories That Watch You Sleep,* against her bent legs. She opened it to the page she had been holding with her index finger. Handwritten words covered both margins. There were no cute pictures of unicorns, no bubbly little hearts above the *i*'s. Instead, letters were slashed into the page like paper wounds.

"Whoa," Alex said. "Is this even the same girl?"

"Only one way to find out," replied Yasmin.

They read it together.

The witch thinks I'm stupid. But she's stupid. She don't know what I've been up to. She don't know how good I've got with the plants.

night fell, the princess realized that she was completely lost. With the first stirrings of true panic, she lifted her lantern and followed the path, praying that it would lead back to the castle.

I figured out how to make a sleeping potion.

In moments, she found herself surrounded by mist-shrouded trees, their skeletal branches perfect for princess snatching. She increased her pace, no longer caring that the hem of her beautiful gown was getting splattered by mud. For the first time in her life, she realized that there were places in the world where not even a princess was safe.

ell. Almost igured out.

I tried to put a few drops in the cat's water but the cat won't drink it because it smells so bad so I forced myself to drink some.

In time, she came to a stone bridge that spanned a narrow stream.

A shadowy figure waited on the other side. The princess thought that it might have been a man, but it was hard to tell. Every time she looked directly at it, her eyes blurred and went out of focus.

"Hello?" the princess asked.

"Hello," the shadow replied.

Slept for a long long time. See witch! ANYONE can do magic!

The beauty of the shadow's voice surprised her. (Its singing voice was even lovelier, though the princess would not have recognized any of the songs.)

SLEEPING POTION

1 part suckleweed
2 parts Gretchen's fury
4 parts yellowglass
pinch of demon's mane

I can't put it in the witch's drink, if she smells it she will know. There must be something I can use to hide it. I will keep trying. Close so close. Then when the witch is asleep I am going to steal her keys and go home.

But. What if she finds me again? What if she drags me back here?

"I think I'm lost," the princess said.

"So it seems."

"I'm looking for the castle."

"That's a long way off."

"Could you take me there?" she asked. "I'm a princess."

"I'm a shadow," said the shadow. "Why don't you cross the bridge?"

"Is that the fastest way to the castle?"

"Cross the bridge and I'll whisper the answer in your ear."

The princess, mesmerized by the shadow's voice, found herself walking across the bridge. As she passed the midway point, she was able to see the shadow more clearly. Its shape kept changing. Sometimes it was a man, sometimes a woman. Sometimes it was something else altogether.

The princess tried to stop walking but the voice lassoed her forward.

"Come on, little princess," the shadow said, opening its arms wide. "Just a few steps more."

I wish I had magic. Then I could turn her into a toad or a snail and laugh at her all day long. But I don't have magic. All I have is this knife.

I HATE HER HATE HER HATE HER

It is not sharp. But it is sharp enough.

Yasmin closed the book.

"Unicorn Girl got *dark*," she said.

"It sounds like she's planning to kill Natacha in her sleep."

"Except obviously she didn't," Yasmin replied.

"That doesn't mean the other part of her plan didn't work. She still could have escaped." He considered this for a moment. "Maybe she just chickened out on the actual stabbing part. Saying it is one thing. Doing it is another. I hate Natacha, but I wouldn't be able to go through with it. You?"

Yasmin thought about it and then shook her head.

"We'll never know what happened for sure," Alex said, "but the important part is that we now have the recipe for a sleeping potion! Do we have those ingredients?"

"Yes," Yasmin said. "They're pretty common, actually. But—"

"So you can make it?"

"Listen, Alex. This girl must have been here a long time ago if Natacha was still making potions. Even if I knew how to make the liquid base I'd need, we don't have the right equipment anymore. Natacha said she got rid of it all when she switched over to essential oils."

"Does it matter?" Alex asked. "Wouldn't the ingredients be the same?"

"I don't know," Yasmin said. "I guess it might work.

These magical recipes usually have to be just right, though. If not, bad things happen, like with the danglers." She twisted the brim of her cap in her hands, thinking it over. "Still, as long as I keep the ratios the same . . . and it's not like Natacha would miss any of the ingredients." She shrugged her shoulders. "It's worth a try, I guess."

"You can do it," Alex said. "I know you can!"

"Even if I do," Yasmin said, "there's still a problem. The smell. It must be from the suckleweed. That stuff stinks something awful, and I have no idea what we could use to mask it. Without that missing ingredient, the oil is useless."

"So we keep looking," Alex said. "Unicorn Girl must have written it down somewhere."

"I'm not so sure about that," Yasmin said. "At this point she seems more in action mode than writing mode. The moment she discovered the missing ingredient I think she'd just move ahead with her plan."

"We have to at least try."

"*I* have to try," Yasmin said. "*You* have to write a story. You only have one left, Alex! Who knows what Natacha will do if you don't—"

Alex grabbed her forearm in excitement.

"A story!" he exclaimed. "That could actually work. You're a genius!"

"Huh?"

"We need to find out the missing ingredient, right? And we know—"

A piercing yowl cut off his sentence.

It was coming from far below them. Alex looked over the railing and saw Lenore materialize on top of the desk.

She looked up at them and yowled again.

"No!" Yasmin exclaimed. "How long has she been down there?"

"The whole time, I bet," Alex said, cursing himself for forgetting about the cat. "She probably heard everything."

"She's going to tell Natacha! We have to stop her!"

They ran down the stairs as fast as they could. Lenore didn't turn invisible as Alex figured she would. Instead, she was doing something to the books they had left on the desk. He couldn't see exactly what without slowing down, and he wasn't sure it mattered. The most important thing was to keep the little spy away from her master.

But why make such a dramatic appearance? he wondered. *Why not just remain invisible and tell Natacha later?*

He had no idea.

"Lenore," Alex said as he finally reached the bottom of the stairs. "I don't know what you heard, but it's not what you think. I was just running story ideas by Yasmin, okay?"

Lenore gave him a look of insulted disbelief: *Just because I'm a cat doesn't make me stupid.*

As Alex moved straight ahead, Yasmin circled around to the back of the desk. The idea wasn't to sneak up on Lenore, who clearly knew she was coming. They were just trying to cut off any exit paths. Then again, Alex wasn't convinced that either one of them would be able to stop Lenore, even if they tried. She might have looked like a lazy housecat, but she was a fierce fighter.

"Lenore," Yasmin began, her voice gentle. "Please. We helped you, remember? Let's be friends."

Behind Alex, the door handle rattled. He spun around just as Natacha burst into the room.

She eyed the two children with triumph.

"Why the guilty looks?" the witch asked.

That's why Lenore started yowling, Alex thought. *She heard Natacha come home. She was calling her to the library, so we would be caught red-handed.*

"We're not doing anything," Yasmin said weakly.

"True," Natacha said, picking up a pencil from the desk. "*You're* not in the nursery tending to my plants." She leveled her gaze on Alex. "And *you're* not writing. So what, exactly, are you two doing?"

The pencil in Natacha's hand transformed into a yellow snake that slithered between her fingers.

"Tell me," she said. "Before I forget to ask nicely."

"Yasmin was helping me with research for a story," Alex said. "I want to make sure I get all the details right."

"Research?" Natacha asked dubiously.

"That's right," Yasmin said, going with it. "Research. A whole lot of research."

"Research about *what*?" Natacha asked.

She kept her eyes glued to Yasmin, waiting for an answer.

"You know," Yasmin said, shifting from foot to foot. "About . . . well, Alex came to me. At breakfast. We had oatmeal. And he asked me—he said—no, he asked, if I could help him learn some things . . ."

"About magic oils," Alex said. He folded his arms across his chest to hide his trembling hands. "I wanted to get all the little details right. Yasmin's the expert."

Natacha's face tightened. The pencil-snake, sensing its master's discomfiture, bared its lead fangs in Alex's direction.

"The *expert*?" Natacha asked. "That girl doesn't know a single thing that I didn't teach her."

"I wouldn't be so sure about that," Alex said. "I think Yasmin might have picked up some really fascinating techniques on her own. Who knows? Maybe she could teach you a thing or two!"

"What?" Natacha snarled, glaring at Yasmin. "She's not even a witch!"

Yasmin shot Alex a nervous look: *What are you doing?*

"True," Alex said in a pacifying tone, stepping between

them. "Obviously Yasmin wasn't my first choice, only I couldn't go to you for research. I want the story to be a surprise! Otherwise what's the point?"

This seemed to mollify Natacha somewhat. The anger that faded from her face, however, was quickly replaced by a fiendish grin.

"You wouldn't be telling me a story, storyteller," she asked, "would you?"

"Of course not."

"We'll see about that," she said. "Lenore!"

The cat leaped gracefully off the desk and landed at Natacha's feet.

"Tell me what these two were really doing."

Alex looked at Yasmin. She was trying to keep her face as impassive as possible, but he could see the panic swirling in her eyes. *What do we do?* he thought. If they ran, they would just be admitting their guilt—and where could they go? On the other hand, if they stayed here and Lenore told Natacha they had been planning their escape . . .

There's no way out of this, Alex thought.

Natacha traced a line in the air from her ear to Lenore's mouth. As she did, a narrow tube of swirling green water appeared. Lenore meowed into the bottom of the tube, over and over again, and tiny bubbles floated through the water and up to the witch's ear.

It's an animal translator, Alex thought.

Unfortunately, Natacha did not look pleased by whatever Lenore was saying. Alex and Yasmin shared a concerned look.

"Really?" the witch asked, her tone more accusatory than surprised. "That can't be right."

More meowing.

"Are you sure?"

Some final meows, more insistent this time, as though Lenore was getting annoyed with her master. Natacha, for her part, looked like she wanted to kick the cat across the room.

"So be it," Natacha said.

She waved the translator out of existence and faced the children.

"Lenore tells me she's been here all morning," Natacha said through gritted teeth, "and that what you just said is the absolute and total truth."

Alex clamped his mouth shut so his jaw didn't fall open in shock.

Lenore lied for us, he thought.

"After all the trouble you two caused with the danglers," Natacha continued, "I decided to make a surprise visit to check up on you. Looks like you've learned your lesson. Now make sure you don't forget it." She reached for the doorknob and then looked back over her shoulder at Alex. "I look forward to your story tonight. Hopefully all that research paid off."

"That particular story isn't finished yet," Alex said. "Maybe tomorrow or the next—"

"Tonight," Natacha said with a threatening glare. "I can't wait."

She left the room.

"I am so confused right now," Yasmin said. "I thought Lenore was making all that noise to tell Natacha what we were up to, but—"

"She heard Natacha come home early," Alex said. "She was warning us to get down from the tower. Less suspicious that way."

"And look at what she did with the books," Yasmin added, gesturing toward a neat stack on the table. "Like total idiots, we left them open to the Unicorn Girl entries. Lenore closed them all so Natacha wouldn't see. She wasn't tattling on us. She was saving us. But why?"

Both children turned toward the cat, who hopped up on the table and lay down as if nothing had happened. Yasmin's ointment had done its work; her wounds were almost entirely healed.

"Because we were kind," Alex said. "And kindness beats cruelty every time."

He reached down and stroked Lenore's head. She let him.

“You’re a prisoner just like us, aren’t you?” Yasmin asked, bending down. “We’re going to escape—or try to, at least.” She rubbed the cat’s stomach. “Do you want to come with us?”

Alex wasn’t sure how many of the words Lenore understood without a magical translator, but it must have been enough. She began to purr.

Alex and Yasmin looked at each other and smiled.

Now they were three.

15

DANGEROUS LIES

Alex hadn't been lying to Natacha; in order to write his next story, he really did need to ask Yasmin some questions about magical oils. By the time they were done, he had filled nearly two pages with notes.

"Why did you make it seem like I know more about this stuff than she does?" Yasmin asked. "We both know that isn't true."

"I wanted to see how she reacted when I questioned her expertise," Alex said. "Have you heard her grill me after I read a story, say I don't know this or I don't know that?"

"Yeah," Yasmin said, stifling a grin. "I've noticed how much that gets under your skin."

"It does not," Alex said. Yasmin raised her eyebrows. "Okay, maybe a little bit."

"More than a little bit."

"The important thing is that Natacha's a know-it-all. And when I claimed you know more than she does, she couldn't take it. She reacted just the way I hoped."

"You *wanted* to get her mad?"

"Yes," Alex said. "Angry people don't think clearly. They let things slip. We can use that to our advantage."

"There's a few disadvantages to getting Natacha mad, too. Like she might lose her temper and turn us into a matching pair of socks."

"I know," Alex said. "But if we really want to escape, we need to start taking some risks."

He explained the rest of his plan. Yasmin listened with growing incredulity.

"I don't know," she said when he had finished. "It *might* work. If we're lucky. But wouldn't it be safer to search the books in the library first? Maybe I was wrong. Maybe Unicorn Girl did write the missing ingredient somewhere."

"Even if she did," Alex said, "it could take weeks for us to find it. So many bad things could happen before then. I might not be able to think of a story. Natacha could wake up on the wrong side of the bed and decide she's tired of both of us. The sooner we get out of here, the better."

"But if Natacha figures out what you're trying to do—"

"She won't," Alex said. "I'll be careful. Like a word ninja."

"You better be," Yasmin said. "Or this is going to be the shortest story you ever told."

After that, Alex settled into his chair and started writing. The story came easily. It turned out that he wasn't suffering from writer's block after all; he just wasn't ready to write his ghost story yet. Once he changed gears the words flowed like running water.

He finished just before dinner.

Yasmin had outdone herself: honey-glazed ham, scalloped potatoes, corn bread, and fresh applesauce. There was far too much food for one person to eat, and Alex knew that afterward he would have to dump most of it into the trash. Natacha didn't eat leftovers, and she refused to allow the children a single bite. It was the worst of her casual cruelties.

As Alex refilled the witch's glass, the succulent smells of the feast teasing his empty stomach, he imagined her taking a sip of lemonade and falling face-first into her potatoes, sound asleep.

The image brought a tiny smile to his lips.

"What's wrong with you?" Natacha snapped, turning in his direction. "Why are you *happy*?"

"Just looking forward to tonight's story," Alex said. "I think you'll like it."

Natacha shrugged and tore off a piece of corn bread.

Alex was no longer surprised by her indifference, though he still found it puzzling. Despite her impressive library, Natacha had given no indication that she truly *loved* stories the way that he did. They were there to serve a purpose, like a hastily prepared meal.

All she cares about is keeping the apartment calm and under control, he thought, *feeding it darkness like you'd toss hunks of meat to a wild beast.*

Alex wished he understood more about the nature of apartment 4E. Why couldn't Natacha use her magic to control it? Did it have a mind of its own? For the most part, the apartment helped Natacha by giving her the extra space she needed and bringing new captives to her door. But there were other times, especially when the apartment was in earthquake mode, that Natacha seemed almost afraid of it.

Perhaps solving this mystery would help them, perhaps not. Right now, Alex had to remain focused on the task at hand. After Natacha finished her second slice of pecan pie, they moved into the living room. Every movement he made seemed forced. Every word he spoke sounded wooden and exaggerated. He felt like a bad actor in a horror movie.

It's just your imagination, he thought. *There's no way the witch has any idea—*

"You're not telling me everything," Natacha said.

Alex nearly dropped the nightbook in his hands. His throat suddenly felt as dry as a sandstorm.

"What are you talking about?" he asked.

"Don't play stupid with me," Natacha said. "You know exactly what I'm talking about."

Alex hesitated, afraid to speak.

"There's a reason you wanted to destroy your nightbooks!" Natacha exclaimed. "Something happened! Something that gave you that final little nudge. Maybe that very same day."

Alex let out a slow sigh of relief. *This isn't about tonight's plan at all*, he thought.

"Nothing happened," Alex said. "I just decided that it was time for a change."

"I wonder if I can make your nose grow like Pinocchio," Natacha said, staring at his face with a thoughtful expression. "I've never tried it before. Something might go terribly wrong." She reached over and poked the tip of his nose. "But you know me. I'm always up for a little experimentation."

Alex swallowed nervously. *Why is she bringing this up now?*

"It's not worth talking about," he said.

Natacha squeezed the arms of her chair and pulled herself forward. She grinned with triumph, her eyes popping out.

"So something *did* happen!" she exclaimed. "You admit it!"

If Alex and the witch had been alone, he would have just told her. Living through that morning again would have been humiliating, but in the end Natacha's opinion didn't really matter to him. The problem was Yasmin. Once she discovered the truth, he was afraid that she wouldn't want to be his friend anymore.

"Tell me," Natacha said. "Now."

"No," Alex said.

Natacha's mouth fell open in a look of such exaggerated surprise that Alex almost laughed. He wondered how long it had been since someone refused her.

"I'm not asking," she said, her face growing flushed like a spoiled child. "You either tell me, or—"

Yasmin shrieked and jumped to her feet.

"You feel that?" she asked.

Natacha gave her a quizzical look. "Feel what?"

"The floor just trembled," Yasmin said. "I think the apartment is about to have one of its earthquakes."

"I didn't feel anything," Natacha said, but there was a slight quiver in her voice. *I was right,* Alex thought. *The apartment* does *frighten her.*

"There!" Yasmin exclaimed. "Another one! I don't think you can feel it because your feet aren't on the floor."

Alex's feet *were* on the floor, and he felt nothing. It

was clear that Yasmin was lying. She had seen that Alex was treading in dangerous waters and made up an entire "earthquake" as a distraction.

"I felt it too, Natacha," Alex said, opening his nightbook. "I should probably start. It feels like it's going to be a bad one."

The witch spun in his direction.

"Then what are you waiting for?" she screeched, clawing nervously at her hair. "Read!"

Alex paused a moment to meet Yasmin's eyes—*thank you*—and began.

NEVERWORM

The Great Monster had terrorized the land for as long as anyone could remember. It swatted away armies and laughed at fire. Nothing could stop it. In desperation, the witches joined forces and cast a special sleeping spell. No one really thought it would work. But it did. The Great Monster closed its eyes and toppled over. A thousand trees fell beneath its weight.

At long last, its reign of terror was over.

The next step should have been to kill the Great Monster before it woke up. After all, the monster was not immortal. It could be slain like any other beast, with spell or sword or spear.

Unfortunately, precious gems grew inside the Great Monster's mouth like minerals in a cave. They would stop growing when the monster took its last breath.

And people are greedy.

Instead of killing the sleeping monster, the witches built a city in its shadow. Over the years, they grew rich and prosperous from the monster's gems. They never went inside the mouth themselves. Each month they selected a young boy, always from a poor family, and tossed him into the gaping maw. Sometimes the boy returned to the city with treasure held high. Most of the time, however, the boy was never seen again. The Great Monster might have been asleep, but it still needed to eat.

In time the original enchantment wore off, but the witches made sure that the Great Monster's slumber continued. Every morning they scaled its body and funneled a powerful sleeping potion down its fifth ear. The recipe for this potion was as old as time itself. Rat bones dissolved in a pitcher plant. Widow orchid. Powdered beetle shells. The most important ingredient, however, was bindweed, a rare plant that grew in swamps and sucked up smells instead of water. Bindweed was the only thing in the world that could hide the powerful stench of the sleeping potion. This was important, because the Great Monster had as many noses as teeth. Without bindweed, the terrible smell of the potion would wake it up.

A thousand years passed in this manner.

And then one day all the bindweed withered and died.

The wisest witches gathered together to pool their knowledge. Was there a different ingredient they could use in place of bindweed? Serpent's tongue? Snail mucus? Charred plugseed? Nothing worked. The potion smelled worse than ever. So the witches called on the great warriors of the city. There was no other choice. They would have to kill the Great Monster, once and for all, before it was too late.

That night, while the warriors sharpened their spears, the baker's daughter entered the Golden Hall.

She was small, both in stature and age, but very, very clever. The other witches had never met her before. She lived in the poor section of the city, where a proper witch never went.

"I've found a replacement for bindweed," the baker's daughter announced. "It'll take the smell away so you can put the Great Monster back to sleep."

"Nonsense," said the eldest witch. "Nothing can replace bindweed."

"Nightberry juice," proclaimed the baker's daughter.

The witches laughed. Nightberries made excellent pie, but they had no magical properties at all.

"Foolish child," said the eldest witch. "You know nothing of real magic."

"Let me prove it to you," said the baker's daughter. "Give me some of your famous sleeping potion."

The witch snapped her fingers and a servant brought out a vial of the potion. It smelled like a dead skunk that had been lying in the sun for days. The girl pinched her nose and withdrew a bottle of violet liquid from her cloak. She poured a drop into the vial.

The smell went away instantly.

"Impossible," the eldest witch said. "Nightberry juice doesn't hold that kind of power!"

She ordered the servant to bring out a second vial of the sleeping potion. The baker's daughter added a drop of liquid from her bottle. The smell vanished again.

The eldest witch was convinced.

"Tell the warriors to stand down!" she announced, snatching the bottle from the girl's hand. "Our problem is solved! The monster will continue to sleep, and we shall mine its gems as always!"

The baker's daughter watched her with a curious expression.

"Perhaps you were hoping for a reward?" the eldest witch asked with a cruel twist of her lips. "If so, you should have kept your ingredient a secret. You could have named your treasure, once you proved it worked. But now that we know it's simple nightberry juice, there's no reason to reward you."

The baker's daughter bowed her head.

"How foolish of me," she said. "I wish I was wise, like a witch."

"On the other hand, we can't have you telling people that you were the one who solved our problem," the witch said. "You will leave at once and never return. A horse and supplies wait for you beyond the city walls. We will tell your parents that you drowned in the river."

"My mother and father are already dead," the baker's daughter said. "As is my brother." There was a sharpness to her voice that had not been there before.

"Even easier, then," said the witch, not interested.

She waved her wand. There was a flash of light, and the baker's daughter found herself on the outskirts of the city. An old gelding was waiting for her, as promised. The girl rode the horse to the top of a large hill a few miles from the city. It was as good a spot as any from which to watch. She sat down in the grass. In the distance, the Great Monster slumbered. The baker's daughter could see its claws from here, as big as trees but far sharper.

She imagined what was happening right now.

No doubt the witches had already made a batch of new potion with the liquid from the girl's bottle. Someone would be pouring the potion into the fifth ear, thinking that she was saving everyone in the entire city . . .

The baker's daughter smiled.

The eldest witch was right. Nightberry juice had no magical properties. But the bottle that the baker's daughter brought to the witches had been filled with more than just nightberry juice. There was a pinch of neverworm in there as well, from the patch that the baker's daughter had found while poisoning all the bindweed. Such a possibility had never occurred to the eldest witch, for who would be mad enough to do such a thing?

Neverworm not only erased the smell of any potion it was added to. It erased its magic as well. In fact, just the tiniest touch of neverworm could undo the most powerful enchantment.

The baker's daughter only wished the rest of her family could be here to see her revenge. Her sweet brother, who had been thrown into the mouth of the Great Monster and never returned. Her poor father, dead of a broken heart, and her mother, who followed him soon afterward.

She missed them with a love both fierce and terrible.

The girl removed a frosted roll from her cloak. She had baked it earlier this morning, using her family's recipe. As the monster awoke and the screams began, she took a tiny bite. It was delicious.

The misting room had dissipated several minutes beforehand, giving Alex a clear view of Natacha's face. She looked livid.

"What. Was. *That*?" she asked.

Alex tried to look as hurt as possible.

"You didn't like it?" he asked. "Really? I wrote it for you! I figured since the story was about magic you might—"

"Why was the witch fooled so easily by a simple . . . *girl*?" she shrieked, leaping to her feet. She poked him in the chest with the long nail of her index finger. "Are you saying that I'm *stupid*? That I'm *gullible*? Is that what you're trying to tell me?"

Natacha was so self-centered that she assumed the story was about her. Alex had hoped this would be the case.

If she's upset, she's more likely to slip up and tell us what we need to know.

Still, he had to be careful. He couldn't push her *too* far.

"It's just a story," Alex said. "I needed a foolish witch in order to make the ending work. She's just make-believe, a character. Obviously, a brilliant witch like you—a witch who knows more about magic than anyone else in the world, a witch so amazing that"—he saw Yasmin give a little shake of her head: *Too much, too much!*—"anyway, *you* never would have fallen for it."

Natacha nodded, drinking it up.

"That's right," she said. "I would have seen right through her."

"You would have tested the potion first," Alex said. "Made sure it actually worked before you sent someone to use it on the monster."

"Obviously," Natacha said.

"And you would have investigated why all the bindweed died to begin with," Alex said. "I mean, the only herb that can erase the smell of a potion suddenly gets wiped out? That's pretty suspicious."

Natacha laughed into the back of her hand.

"What?" Alex asked.

"Bindweed," she said. "Yasmin tell you to use that? That part of your 'research'?"

Alex brightened.

"You noticed!" he exclaimed. "I thought you'd like the story better if I used real magical ingredients instead of just making them up. Yasmin was a big help."

"Neverworm isn't real, obviously," Yasmin admitted. "And I had to guess at what ingredients might be used in a sleeping potion, but I'm pretty sure that recipe could work." She ignored Natacha's dismissive chortle. "And I know for a *fact* that bindweed conceals magical odors. It was Claire who told me that, and she was an *expert*."

Yasmin glared at Natacha in defiance, as though daring the witch to contradict her.

The witch stopped laughing.

"There's only one expert, girl," Natacha said. "Me. And I'm here to tell you that bindweed is good for exactly one thing: combining magical ingredients that would otherwise be incapable of working together. It's magic glue, nothing more."

Yasmin shook her head in amusement, as though Natacha were a poor student who had just added when she should have subtracted.

"No, no, no," she said. "That's *totally* wrong."

Flames erupted in Natacha's eyes.

"What did you say?" she asked.

Alex sent a warning glance in Yasmin's direction. They had planned to get Natacha upset, but not *that* upset. One more word and she might find herself a porcelain figurine.

Yasmin ignored him.

"Bindweed makes the foulest magical odor vanish," Yasmin said, stubbornly crossing her arms. "I've seen it work."

"Impossible," Natacha said, but there was the slightest flicker of doubt in her tone.

She's not as sure of herself as she seems, Alex thought.

"Remember that order of beauty oil you had me make a few weeks back?" Yasmin asked. "The shrew feet were past their prime, and the whole batch ended up stinking really bad. I added lavender, lemongrass, all the usual, hoping to cancel it out, but nothing worked. So I threw in a few sprigs of bindweed." Yasmin snapped her fingers. "Ta-da! No more odor."

"You're wrong!" Natacha exclaimed. Her uncertainty had passed; now there was only anger. "Bindweed doesn't do that!"

"Except it did," Yasmin replied. "So I really don't see what other explanation—"

Alex clapped his hands together, as though he had just thought of a great idea.

"Hey, I know!" he suggested. "Maybe you got your ingredients confused. You thought it was bindweed, but it was . . . I don't know . . . what takes away smell?"

He shrugged and turned to Natacha for assistance. The witch, clearly warming to the idea that Yasmin had made a mistake, was quick to respond.

"Cinaroot," she said. "It's the only thing that would have actually *worked*."

Alex nodded, as though this was only of passing interest, but there were fireworks exploding in his head.

Got it! Got it! Got it!

"Oh!" Yasmin exclaimed, smacking herself in the forehead. "This is embarrassing. I had just used cinaroot in a different oil, and I guess . . . I might have gotten it confused with bindweed."

"They don't even look anything alike," Natacha said,

her air of superiority returning in full force. "How stupid can you be?"

"You're right," Yasmin said.

"Of course I'm right," Natacha replied, raising her chin high. "I'm the witch!" She snapped her fingers in Alex's direction. "Well, what are you doing? Correct your story before you forget! And if you need to do any more research in the future, you come to me. Got it?"

"Got it," Alex said, removing a pencil from his pocket. He erased his first use of "bindweed" and then looked up with a shy smile. "Does *cinaroot* start with an *s* or a *c*? I just want to make sure I get it right."

16

A PAIR OF RED EYES

After a quick breakfast, the two children donned their goggles and entered the nursery. It was the first time that Alex had been back since the incident with the danglers, and he was amazed at all the work Yasmin had done. Shattered black lights had been replaced, overturned plants restored to their rightful position. Luminous leaves and glowing stems created a brightly lit path through the darkness.

Unlike the last time he had been here, the nursery was quiet and peaceful.

Why does that night seem so long ago? Alex wondered.

They moved quickly, Yasmin stopping every so often to gather an ingredient she needed. At one point she handed Alex a pair of scissors to hold. She didn't ask him to hold them, nor did she need to.

Inspired by this subtle gesture of friendship, Alex

decided to risk a question that had been on his mind.

"So where do you live?" Alex asked. "In the real world."

"Why do you want to know?" Yasmin asked. The old caution had crept into her voice.

"Sorry," Alex said, a little hurt. "I know you don't like to talk about your old life. I just thought that maybe things had changed."

She touched his hand in the darkness.

"It's not that I don't want to tell you, Alex," Yasmin said. "It's just . . . it hurts too much to talk about it. I miss my family. A lot. But they're like a wound that hasn't healed. If I don't think about it, the pain is bearable, but the moment I talk about home, or say their names—I remember how bad it hurts. It has nothing to do with you."

"I get that," Alex said, relieved. "I just wanted to see how close we lived to each other." He paused, then added softly, "You know, in case we ever want to hang out or something. After."

"Oh," Yasmin said. "You really think we're going to get out of here?"

"Unicorn Girl did it," Alex said. "Why not us?"

Yasmin considered this for a long time.

"Thirty-Third Street," she finally said, looking over her shoulder. Her face was tinted mauve from a nearby fern. "Just off Parsons."

Alex smiled. It was too far for him to walk, but there

was a bus stop right on the corner.

"That'll work," he said.

They took a sharp left down a narrow hallway that he hadn't noticed before. After a short walk, they came to a heavy curtain identical to the one near the entrance to the nursery. Yasmin held it open for him. As he entered the next room, Alex felt Lenore brush past his legs. Until that moment he'd had no idea that she had even followed them, but he was glad.

She should be here for this, he thought. *She's one of us.*

"You can take your goggles off now," Yasmin said, letting the curtain close behind them. She removed her own goggles and reached for something behind Alex.

Click.

Work lights buzzed to life. They were regular lights, not black lights, and Alex squinted against the unexpected brightness. After his eyes had a chance to readjust, he saw that he was in a simple room with a concrete floor and four identical silver machines.

"Oil distillers," Yasmin said. "You put the magic herbs inside, steam sucks out all the good stuff and turns it into a few drops of essential oil. Pretty cool, right?"

Each distiller was split into two vats with dials and tubes between them. The bottom one was fat and wide and looked like it could hold a lot of liquid. Above it was a tall cylinder on a metal stand that reminded Alex of a pipe from an old church organ.

Three of the distillers bubbled and chugged and occasionally released puffs of copper-hued smoke into the air. Alex stepped closer to one of them and held his hand a few inches shy of its surface. Waves of heat tingled his skin.

"Don't touch it!" Yasmin exclaimed. "You'll get a nasty burn."

Alex pulled his hand back.

"What's this one making right now?" he asked.

Yasmin consulted a notebook hanging off a small stepladder.

"Popularity oil." She pointed to the other two machines in turn. "Hair-growing oil. Acne oil."

"To give someone acne or take it away?"

"Beats me," Yasmin said. "I just follow the recipe."

She crossed the room to a wooden workbench. Long trays held beakers of all shapes and sizes. There were also several knives crusted with old plant matter.

"How long will it take?" Alex asked, bending down to feed Lenore a handful of Froot Loops. She gobbled them up quickly and then nudged his pocket with her head, wanting more. Alex obliged.

"We can't do anything yet," Yasmin said, hanging the herbs from hooks above the workbench. "We have to let these dry overnight." She switched on a small heating unit beneath the herbs; warm air blew upward. "In the morning,

I can set them up in the distiller. Figure six hours in the machine . . . we should be ready to go by tomorrow night."

"Assuming I can think of a story," Alex said. "Only two left. After tonight I'm all out."

"Why bother writing anything new?" Yasmin asked, washing her hands in a slop sink. "Natacha is going to drink the sleeping oil during dinner. She'll be asleep before you have to read anything."

"We don't know if it's going to work right away," Alex said. "The original recipe was for a potion. We're changing it to an oil. What if it takes a little while to kick in? We want everything to seem as normal as possible while we wait."

"A single drop of oil is super concentrated," Yasmin said, bending down to check a temperature gauge outside one of the distillers. "My guess is it will work even faster than a potion." She thought about this for a moment. "Huh," she said. "I hope it's not *too* strong. We don't want to kill her."

"Yeah," Alex said. "I want to get out of here, but I don't want to murder anyone."

"Oh no," Yasmin said, shaking her head. "I would feel bad, too—well, sort of—but that's not the reason we don't want to kill her. Think about it. What happens if you're wrong about her bedroom door? What if it doesn't lead outside?"

"It does," Alex said. "I'm positive."

"Then what if that particular bonekey has some sort of magical protection," Yasmin said. "And Natacha is the only one who can use it."

"Oh," Alex said. He hadn't thought of that possibility. "I see what you mean now. If something happens to Natacha, we might be trapped in the apartment forever. Eventually we'd just starve to death."

He shuddered as his overactive imagination sent him horrifying images of starvation. Lenore, sensing a sudden need for comfort, brushed against his legs.

"That was always my argument with Eli, whenever he said we should try to kill her," Yasmin said. "Not that he listened in the end. I do have an idea, though. What if we put this off a few days and test the oil first, make sure we know what it does?"

"Didn't you just say it could kill Natacha?" Alex asked.

"Not test it on *us*," Yasmin said. She eyed Lenore. "But there might be another living creature that could help us out. I mean, the oil probably works fine, so it'll just end up being a nice nap. . . ."

Lenore looked from Yasmin to Alex with an expression of disbelief: *Is she seriously suggesting this?*

Alex picked up the cat and held her close.

"Not going to happen," he said.

"Fine," said Yasmin. "Then we'll just have to go into this blind. But yeah, you should probably have a story ready, just in case. We don't really know what to expect. Weren't you working on a ghost one? That sounded pretty good."

"Still stuck," Alex said.

"Want to kick some ideas around?"

Alex hesitated, but only for a moment. Time was running out, and he needed all the help he could get.

"That would be great," he said.

"Let's see," Yasmin said. "My Language Arts teacher said you're supposed to write what you know. So . . . ever have any scary experiences?"

"Well, this one time I was captured by a witch."

"Besides that."

"Okay," Alex said, taking a deep breath. "There is one thing. I've never really told anyone about it, though."

Yasmin took a seat on the floor and motioned for Alex to do the same.

"All we need is a campfire," she said. "Come on. Tell me."

"So, I was waiting for the seven train with my parents—not on one of the outdoor platforms, but down in the Main Street station. There was a pretty bad snowstorm that day, so there weren't a lot of people out and about. The platform was empty. My parents were having some kind of serious talk with John, so I wandered away, mostly out of boredom. I must have been, like, I don't know, four or five at the time. I crept down to the end of the platform, just to see if the subway was coming, and deep in the tunnel I saw these two red lights in the distance. At first I figured it was just a pair of signals or something." Alex swallowed slowly. "But then they blinked."

Yasmin's eyes widened.

"What happened next?" she asked, transfixed.

"The eyes moved," Alex said. "They got closer to the edge of the tunnel, to the border between the darkness and the light. I knew I should go back to my parents. But . . . those red eyes hypnotized me." Alex rose to his feet, acting out his movements in the story. "I got closer to the darkness. Closer. It was like I wasn't even controlling my own feet anymore."

He knelt down, his face close to Yasmin's now.

"And then . . . the thing with the red eyes . . . it whispered something," he said.

Yasmin leaned forward.

"What?" she asked.

"Yasmin!"

She screamed, falling backward.

"Got you," Alex said, laughing hard. "I got you so good."

"You are the worst!" she exclaimed, smacking him hard on the arm. For a second Alex was afraid she was actually mad, but then he saw the huge smile on her face. "Seriously, we are no longer friends."

"You have no choice," Alex said. "I'm the only one here."

"Lenore," Yasmin said, turning toward the cat. "Would

you like to be my friend? My *only* friend?"

Lenore gave both of them a strange look, as though she would never understand humans, and disappeared.

"You just got rejected by a cat," Alex said.

"It kind of hurts," Yasmin said. "You know, even though you're a total jerk and I'm going to hate you forever, you did give me an idea. That story was scary because it was so *normal*. Everyone knows what a subway station is like at night. I could picture it in my head. So maybe you should write about something in your life. It doesn't even need to be anything scary at first. You can just dress it up that way."

"Take something real and make it creepy," Alex said, nodding his head. "A lot of famous horror authors do that."

"Exactly," Yasmin said. "Like, imagine you were going to write a story about someone you know. Who would you write about?"

"My brother," Alex said without hesitation.

"Really?" Yasmin asked in surprise. "From what you said, I didn't think you guys were close."

"We're not," said Alex. "That's the point. Every story needs conflict. And every moment with John? Conflict."

"Maybe start with him, then."

"Brothers who don't get along," Alex said, rolling it over in his head. "And then add some of my other ideas. See what works best together."

"Like cooking," Yasmin replied, smiling. "Maybe we're not so different after all. Except you're still a jerk and I'm really nice. That's why Lenore likes me better."

"Lenore does *not* like you better."

"Enough yapping," she said, shoving him playfully toward the exit. "You need to get to work."

By the end of the day, Alex had started four different stories about brothers who couldn't get along. None of them were right. He began to wonder if the whole thing was a dead end.

What am I going to do?

As if they didn't have enough problems, Natacha seemed to be onto them. She barely said a word all evening, except to ask Alex for his nightbook. She examined it with surprising thoroughness, even pausing to read a page here and there, and then handed it back to him with a knowing look, as though a suspicion had been confirmed.

As Alex read his story, about a girl who gets a strange pet for her birthday, he felt her eyes watching him the entire time.

She knows!

But later, as he lay in bed, too worried to sleep, Alex changed his mind.

If Natacha knew what we were up to, why didn't she

do something about it right there and then? I'm just seeing shapes in the shadows, that's all.

That made him feel a little better, but it didn't help him with his other problem.

The story.

What if I can't think of anything? he thought, heart racing. *Will Natacha have time to turn me into one of her porcelain figurines before the sleeping oil kicks in?*

He stared at the mattress above him, cycling through ideas like channels on a TV.

Eyeglasses that let you see invisible monsters. A gravestone that tells you when you die. A comic-book shop that—

And then it hit him.

"There you are!" he exclaimed.

Alex burst into laughter. He couldn't help it. The perfect idea had been in front of him the entire time.

There was no sense trying to go back to sleep. His mind was awake and eager to work. Alex practically skipped to the library and hopped into his chair. The words came easily, as he knew they would.

By late afternoon, he had finished his story.

17

PROBLEMS AND SOLUTIONS

Yasmin somehow found the time to make another incredible meal that night: fried fish with sweet potato fries and homemade coleslaw. Alex pinched his fingers together, intending to steal just one tiny fry. Yasmin slapped his hand away.

"Fine," Alex whispered. "But the moment she falls asleep, I'm eating these. Where did you learn to cook like this, anyway?"

"My sito," Yasmin said.

"Oh," Alex said. He remembered Yasmin's story, the cruel way that the apartment had captured her. "I'm sorry. I didn't mean—"

"It's okay," Yasmin said. Alex was surprised to see that she was smiling. "I don't know why, but it doesn't hurt as much, thinking about her now. Sito and I used to spend hours in the kitchen together. She was the only one who supported my dream." Yasmin's cheeks grew red. "I want to open my own restaurant when I grow up," she added shyly.

"Cool!" Alex said. "What kind?"

Yasmin's face lit up.

"Vegetarian," she said. "Mixed menu—American and Middle Eastern. And there's going to be a baseball theme. All the waiters and waitresses will wear uniforms, and—this is my favorite part—customers get a pennant that they can stick in the middle of their table, like a flag. Whatever their favorite team is."

"Even Yankees fans?"

"I suppose," Yasmin said, rolling her eyes.

"That sounds amazing."

There was an awkward pause. Both of them knew that they were killing time, nervously putting off the next step in their plan. After that, there would be no turning back.

They stared at Natacha's glass, filled to the brim with lemonade.

"You should do the honors," Alex said.

Yasmin withdrew a tiny vial from her pocket.

"It's still a little warm."

"The lemonade's cold," Alex said, reaching for a spoon. "We'll mix it up. She'll never know."

"Okay," Yasmin said, slowly tilting the vial over the rim

of the glass. "Here goes nothing."

A drop of clear oil fell into the lemonade. Alex waited for it to sink into the liquid and disperse, but instead the oil spread across the surface, leaving a greasy scrim that stretched from one edge of the glass to the other.

Alex stirred the lemonade. All that did was spread the oil around and make it even more obvious.

"Why isn't this working?" Alex asked. The spoon clinked against the glass, faster and faster, in tune to his growing frustration. "Is it because it's magic?"

Yasmin clapped a palm to her forehead.

"It's not a magic thing," she said. "It's a chemistry thing. Oil doesn't mix with water. I'm such an idiot!"

Alex stopped stirring. The oil settled to the surface. There was no way to miss it.

"It's not your fault," he said. "I didn't think of it either."

"Maybe she won't notice," suggested Yasmin.

Alex shook his head and poured the ruined lemonade into the sink.

"We're going to have to think of something else," he said. "We can't give this to Natacha."

"Can't give what to Natacha?"

While they were talking, the witch had entered the kitchen behind them. Alex had no idea how long she had been there, what she had overheard. From the corner of his eye he saw that Yasmin still had the vial of sleeping oil in her hand. She kept her back to Natacha, shielding the vial from view.

"Well?" Natacha asked, stepping forward. "What can't you give me?"

"Your sweet potato fries," Yasmin said, smiling over her shoulder. "Not without paprika!"

Yasmin was not a neat cook, and the kitchen counter was a mess: carving board, garlic peels, bread crumbs, knives, spatulas, eggshells, and half a dozen spice jars. In one smooth movement, she picked up the paprika and hid the vial behind a large container of oregano. It wasn't a great hiding spot by any means, but right now it was the best they could do.

Yasmin sprinkled the fries with paprika.

"That's better," she said. "All set now!"

She carried Natacha's dinner into the dining room while Alex poured a fresh glass of lemonade. He thought about trying to add another drop of oil—*maybe it will be less noticeable if I don't stir it this time*—but Natacha was still standing in the doorway, watching him.

"Let's go, storyteller," she said. "You and I have something important to discuss tonight, and I'm itching to begin."

There was a dangerous gleam in her eyes. Alex felt his body grow cold.

"Coming," he said.

Without giving the vial another look, he walked past Natacha and into the dining room. Yasmin was standing in the corner, hands folded behind her back. She looked like she was doing her best not to cry. Alex knew how she felt.

Their plan was ruined.

"Sit," Natacha said, indicating the chair next to hers.

Alex hesitated, unsure if he had heard her correctly. He had never sat at the dining room table before.

"I don't understand," he said.

Natacha flicked her fingers and the chair jerked backward, scraping against the floor. Invisible hands shoved Alex into the seat.

"You don't have to understand," Natacha said. "That's the joy of being a child. You just have to do as you're told."

She sat at the head of the table and tossed a fry in her mouth.

"Paprika," she said, nodding with approval. "Nice touch."

Natacha seemed to be in a good mood. Alex didn't like that. At least when she was angry he knew what to expect.

"Have you been enjoying your stay here?" Natacha asked him, as though she was a concierge inquiring about his resort experience.

"Not really," said Alex.

"I disagree," replied Natacha. "I know you love sharing

your stories—there's no use denying it. And lately, I can't help but notice that you've developed a friendship with that one over there." She nodded her head in Yasmin's direction. "You've tried to hide it from me. That was smart. But unlike the witch in that awful story you read me the other night, I'm not so easily fooled."

Natacha took a large gulp of her lemonade and wiped her mouth clean with the back of her hand.

"It's all right," she said. "It's better that the two of you have become friends. That will make tonight's lesson even more effective." She leaned forward. "Which brings me to my next question: Is there something you'd like to tell me, storyteller?"

Natacha studied his face. *What do I say?* Alex wondered, shifting in his seat. If she knew that they were planning to escape, things might go easier if he came clean now. But if she didn't know, and this was only a bluff . . .

He glanced over the witch's shoulder at Yasmin, hoping for some guidance.

"Don't look at her," Natacha snapped. "She's not part of this conversation. This is between me and you, witch and storyteller. I'll ask you again. What have you been doing every day?"

"Writing," Alex said.

"Liar!" Natacha screamed. "If that had been the case, you would have finished *dozens* of stories by now. But you haven't. You've been reading me your old stories instead."

Alex stared at her, slack-jawed.

Is that what she's so mad about? he thought, with something approaching relief. *Maybe this isn't about our escape plan after all.*

"How did you know?" he asked, happy to keep the conversation on this track.

"All your old stories are in pen," Natacha said. "Every single one. What little you've written since you've gotten here is in pencil. There aren't any pens in the library."

Alex winced, mad at himself for not using the pen in his bag to keep his writing consistent. It was as careless an error as not capitalizing the first letter of a sentence.

"I'm sorry," he said. "I meant to write more, but I haven't been able to concentrate. I miss my family. But I'm getting better. I've written two stories in the last few days."

"Not good enough," Natacha said. She rose from her seat and opened the door of the china cabinet. "If you keep at this pace, you're going to run out of stories in no time flat, and that won't do. A little inspiration is in order. Something to help you understand the consequences if you don't take your writing duties more seriously." As Natacha talked, she carefully slid one figurine to the right, another to the left. *Are they still alive?* Alex wondered, his stomach churning. *Can they feel her fingers wrapped around their bodies?* "What you need," the witch said, "is an example to set you on the straight and narrow."

Natacha stood back from the cabinet and grinned with malicious delight. She had made just enough room for one more figurine.

That's where Yasmin will go, Alex realized with a rush of horror. *Natacha's glad we've become friends because she knows how much more it will hurt me when I lose her.*

He could see from Yasmin's terrified expression that she had come to the same conclusion.

"I hear what you're saying," Alex said. "Loud and clear. I'll write a story a day. Two stories! You don't have to hurt her."

Natacha slammed her fist against the table. The glass of lemonade overturned, spilling its contents across the table.

"I'm not finished!" she exclaimed with barely restrained rage. "Maybe an example would do the trick, like I said. But there's a second possibility. Maybe it's *you,* Alex Mosher. You've caused nothing but trouble since you've gotten here. There are other storybooks constantly being written, ones that aren't in my library. You can be replaced. It's convenient growing my own stories—like owning a vegetable garden—but all you really do is save me a trip to the bookstore."

She gazed back and forth between the two children while making a clicking noise with her tongue.

"The truth of the matter is I haven't decided which one of you to get rid of yet," Natacha said. "I'll make my decision while you read your story." She started to close the cabinet door and then stopped. "I guess I'll just leave this open for now."

Natacha sat back down and took a bite of her fish, chewing it with a displeased look. She nodded toward her overturned glass.

"Get me more lemonade! This fish is dry."

Alex took the glass with trembling hands and entered the kitchen, his thoughts swirling. *She's going to turn one of us into a statue! What do I do?* He had to figure out a plan now, while he was alone. *How can I stop her?*

He looked down at the empty glass in his hands.

I have to risk it.

If Alex didn't do anything, he—or Yasmin—would be sitting on a shelf by bedtime. But if he put another drop of oil in the lemonade, there was the slightest chance that Natacha might take a sip without noticing it.

Maybe the oil works superfast, he thought. *It might put her to sleep the moment it touches her lips.*

It wasn't much, but a slight chance was better than no chance at all.

He started to fill the glass with lemonade and then stopped. *Maybe it will mix together better if I put the oil in the glass first,* he thought. *It's worth a shot, at least.*

Alex reached for the vial behind the oregano container.

It wasn't there.

No, he thought. *That's impossible.* He frantically searched the entire counter, knocking over a jar of basil and spilling dried mint from a loosely capped bottle onto the floor.

The sleeping oil was gone.

After dinner, Alex lumbered into the living room, too stunned to speak. *Natacha took the oil,* he thought, taking his seat. *It's the only explanation.* She hadn't left the dining room at any point, but so what? Making a single vial disappear would be child's play for a witch. He watched Natacha ease into her chair and start up the oil diffuser. Her true age remained a mystery, but surely after being alive for so long she needed to find new ways to relieve her boredom.

She's probably known about our plan from the beginning, Alex thought, taking his seat. *Toying with us is her idea of fun.*

He turned to Yasmin, wondering if she had any brilliant ideas, but she looked despondent. She had seen the vial was missing while clearing the table. They hadn't been able to talk about it, but Alex figured that she had come to the same conclusion as him.

Natacha took a huge breath of blue mist and gazed at Alex expectantly.

"Make this fast, storyteller," she said. "We have a busy night in front of us."

He opened his nightbook.

We were so close to escaping, he thought.

Alex had written, on more than one occasion, about monsters who tore their victims' still-beating hearts from their chests. Now he knew what it felt like.

With a trembling voice, he started to read.

THE TOP BUNK

When Keith learned that they were getting a new bunk bed, there was no doubt in his mind that he would be the one sleeping on top. After all, Keith was in the fifth grade, and his brother, Scott, was in kindergarten.

A normal little brother would have seen the logic in that.

Scott was not normal.

"Why should you get the top bunk and not me?" he asked. "It's not fair!"

Keith didn't bother to explain. He knew that it would make no difference. To Scott, things that happened the way he wanted them to, such as getting every single present on his Christmas list, were "fair." Disappointing events, such as losing a round of Super Smash Bros., were "not fair."

"You can have the top bunk in a few years," Keith said. "After that I'll move to my own room and—"

"Not fair!" Scott exclaimed. "I want the top bunk now!"

Keith smiled patiently, though inside he wanted to scream at the little brat, something that he wished his parents would do more often. If he lost his temper now, however, Scott would only burst into tears and run to Mom.

Is that his plan? Keith wondered. *Is he trying to get me in trouble?*

No one else would believe that a five-year-old could be so manipulative. Then again, no one else understood Scott as well as Keith did.

"Please," Scott begged. His upper lip quivered in that maddening way that adults found irresistible. "Could I please, please, please have the upper bunk?"

Keith looked into his brother's big blue eyes, shiny with tears.

"No," Keith said. "It's mine."

Scott's eyes hardened. The tears stopped. He gave him the wicked smile that he reserved only for his brother. Keith thought of it as his real-Scott smile.

"We'll see about that," he said.

In the days leading up to the bed's delivery, Scott was a perfect little angel. He ate all his vegetables. He begged for stories and kisses instead of video games. He left tiny, heart-shaped cards on his parents' pillows each night.

And then, the night before the bed arrived, he struck the final blow.

"I'm so small," Scott said at dinner while finishing the last of his brussels sprouts. "At school some of the other kids make fun of me."

"What kids?" Mom asked. "I'll email the teacher and—"

"I don't want to get anyone in trouble," Scott said. "I just wish I was big, that's all."

His upper lip began to do its thing, quivering in that whimpering half cry.

"What is it, sweetie?" Mom asked, already lost.

"I know I can't be big," Scott said between tears. "But maybe I could feel big. Like, if I slept in the upper bunk, like a big boy would do. I think that would make me feel just a little bit better."

Their parents exchanged a look of consideration. It was just long enough for Scott to glance in Keith's direction. He smiled his real-Scott smile.

The next morning, Keith steeled himself for bad news. He was used to Scott getting his own way, and he never argued when it happened. That was just the way things worked.

It was the bed's assembly directions that saved the day.

They stated, in glorious red ink, that kids six and under should sleep on the bottom bunk. Scott whined and pleaded and argued, but while their parents routinely gave in to his demands when it came to playdates and screen time, they refused to budge on matters of safety.

That night, Keith triumphantly claimed the top bunk, while Scott was forced to sleep a lame foot and a half off the ground.

"It's not fair," Scott mumbled after the lights had been turned off.

"It's totally fair and you know it," Keith said.

"Can I sleep in the top bunk?" Scott asked. "Pleaasssee."

"No," Keith said. And then, unable to resist, he added, "The top bunk is for big kids only."

"Not fair," Scott said.

"Whatever," Keith said. "Go to sleep."

Keith figured that would be the end of it. He was wrong.

"Can I sleep in the top bunk?" Scott asked the moment Keith's head touched his pillow the following night. "It's not fair. Let me sleep in the top bunk."

Keith said no, but that didn't seem to matter to Scott. He asked again and again, long into the night. Keith hardly got any sleep at all.

He told his parents the next morning.

"Have a little patience," their father said, the tone of his words implying that Keith was at fault. "In a couple of weeks the poor little guy will forget all about it."

Except Scott, of course, wouldn't let it go. The talking was bad enough. But then, about a week later, Scott found an old broom handle and began poking the bottom of Keith's thin mattress. It didn't hurt. Scott didn't have the strength to press that hard. But it made sleeping impossible.

"Can I sleep in the top bunk?" Scott asked. "Just for one night. Pleeaassee."

Keith was tempted to say yes, just to get a good night's rest, but he knew it would be a mistake. Once Scott slept in the top bunk, it would prove to their parents that it was perfectly safe.

After that, Keith wouldn't have a chance. Scott would win.

The strange thing was, Keith didn't even particularly like sleeping on the top bunk. It was hotter up there, and the ceiling felt like it was pressing down on him. If Scott had been a different sort of kid, Keith probably would have let him have it. But Scott was what he was, and Keith refused to give him his way.

Then Scott died.

It was a stupid way to die, running after a ball like that. It wasn't even his favorite ball, just a moldy old thing that Scott had found under their stoop. He had been tossing it aimlessly against their garage door while Keith—on "Scott duty" as his parents put it—sat on their front steps. When the ball skipped into the street Keith instantly saw the speeding car, Scott's headlong dash toward the road, their inevitable impact.

"Scott!" he screamed, rising from the steps. "Stop!"

A normal kid would have stopped.

Scott was not a normal kid.

The night after the funeral, Keith thought about his brother while lying in bed. The little guy hadn't been all bad. Keith remembered a picture that Scott had drawn in preschool:

stick figures of two brothers, one big and one small, standing beneath a shining sun.

He fell asleep with tears in his eyes.

Keith was awoken by the opening of the bedroom door. It was the squeakiest in the house. His dad always meant to oil the hinges but never got around to it.

"Dad?" Keith mumbled, still groggy. "Mom?"

They hadn't spoken to him much since the accident. They had said all the right things, of course—it's not your fault, there's nothing you could have done, we love you—but what he really wanted was for them to take him in their arms like he was a little boy again. Only then would he truly believe that they didn't blame him for Scott's death.

The door creaked open even wider. From Keith's elevated vantage point, he would have been able to see his dad's or mom's head as they entered the room. He saw no one, leaving only two possibilities. Either the door had opened on its own, or whoever had opened it was a lot smaller than an adult.

Footsteps scampered across the carpet. Blankets rustled as someone settled into the bottom bunk.

Keith remained perfectly still. An invisible weight seemed to be pressing down on him. He wanted to shout for his mom or dad, but it suddenly required all his energy just to keep breathing.

"Keith," a quiet voice whispered beneath him. "Can I have the top bunk?"

Keith tried to scream but all that came out was a soft whimper. He was too terrified to leave his bed. If he did, he would have to go past the bottom bunk.

He would have to see.

"Scott," Keith whispered. "Is that you?"

"Give me the top bunk."

It was his brother's voice all right, only hoarser, as though Scott had been screaming.

This isn't happening, Keith thought. *Scott's dead. This is a nightmare. It's only a—*

Something jabbed him in the back. Keith figured it was the broom handle, only Scott had never been able to push it this hard before.

"It's not fair," Scott whispered, his voice closer now. He was standing on the lower mattress. "I want the top bunk."

"I'm sorry," Keith said. A foul stench had suddenly filled the room. "I'm so sorry about what happened."

Something jabbed him again, harder this time. The mattress lifted into the air for a moment before crashing back down onto its frame.

"Can I sleep on the top bunk?" Scott asked. "Pleeeaaase."

The force of this last word seemed to puncture something within Scott's body. Air hissed like a leaking balloon.

"Please," Scott repeated.

Keith could hear the desperation and fear in his brother's voice.

He's all alone, Keith thought. *He might not even understand what's happening to him.*

"If I let you sleep in the top bunk," Keith asked quietly. "Will you go?"

There was a long pause. The lower bunk squeaked as Scott shifted his weight from foot to foot. Keith heard dirt and pebbles patter to the mattress.

"You'll never see me again," Scott said. "Pinkie promise."

"All right," Keith said. "You can have the top bunk. Tonight only." He hesitated, not wanting to leave the false armor of his blankets, but he knew that there was no other way. "I'll come down the ladder and go. I'm not going to turn around. I'm not going to look."

Scott didn't say a word.

Before Keith could lose his nerve, he threw off the covers and settled his left foot on the ladder, staring straight ahead at the bedroom wall as he descended the rungs.

Second step.

Third step.

A hand grabbed his ankle.

It was cold and small but strong enough to jerk him off his feet. Keith crashed to the floor. He turned over. A familiar figure crouched over him in the darkness, perched on the edge of the bottom bunk like a gargoyle. It craned its head forward into a beam of moonlight shining through the window, and Keith saw a face crusted with dirt and mud that didn't even look like his brother anymore.

"It's not fair," he said in his raspy voice. "How come you get to live and I don't?"

Keith had no time to scream. His brother pounced from the bottom bunk and landed on top of him.

Mrs. Bloch woke up early the next morning, anxious to set things right. They'd been so devastated by Scott's death that they'd completely ignored their oldest son. *Knowing Keith, he probably blames himself*, Mrs. Bloch thought, her heart aching for their quiet, sensitive child. *He's mourning, too. I need to be there for him.*

When she entered the bedroom, Keith was still asleep in the top bunk. There was a peculiar smell in the room, like food that had gone bad. She would clean that up later. Right now, Mrs. Bloch just wanted to see her son.

She stood on the bottom step of the ladder and stared down at him, sleeping peacefully. He had his arm wrapped around one of Scott's stuffed dogs. *He must miss him so much*, Mrs. Bloch thought, stroking his curly blond hair.

Keith's eyes opened.

Mrs. Bloch gasped in shock. Keith had his father's eyes: a deep, solemn brown. But now they looked bright blue, like . . .

Scott's, she thought.

Then Keith blinked and she saw that his eyes were the same brown that they had always been. Mrs. Bloch decided that the exhaustion was making her see things that weren't really there.

"I was so scared, Mommy," Keith whispered, wrapping his arms around her. His voice seemed higher-pitched than before.

Mrs. Bloch held him tight. It had been a long time since Keith had hugged her, and this uncharacteristic show of affection filled her with joy.

"I'm sorry," Mrs. Bloch said, tears coming freely now. "We should have been there for you. But everything is going to be okay now."

They held each other for a long time. When they parted, Keith looked up at her with wide eyes. His upper lip quivered.

"I like the top bunk," he said.

Alex closed the nightbook and looked over at Natacha. Despite everything, he was still curious if she had liked the story or not.

Her eyes were closed.

"Natacha?" Alex asked.

No response. He put his ear next to the invisible wall and heard a gentle, rhythmic snoring.

"What are you doing?" Yasmin asked, watching him with a befuddled expression. From her vantage point, she couldn't see Natacha's face.

"She's asleep," Alex said.

"No way," replied Yasmin, springing from the love seat. She cupped her hands to her eyes and peered through the blue mist. "Natacha never fell asleep during one of your stories before. This can't be a coincidence."

"It has to be connected to the sleeping oil," Alex agreed, hope rising. "But how?"

"Natacha!" Yasmin exclaimed, banging on the walls of the misting room.

"What are you doing?" Alex asked, grabbing her arm.

"We need to see if this is a magic sleep or a regular sleep, before we do anything stupid," replied Yasmin. She screamed at the top of her lungs, "WAKE UP!"

Natacha didn't stir. No question about it: This wasn't a normal type of sleep.

"The sleeping oil worked," Yasmin said in astonishment.

"But how? We never gave it to her."

"Maybe there was still a little of it left on her lemonade glass," Alex suggested. "You said it was super concentrated."

"She's totally out, though," Yasmin said, examining Natacha from all angles. "Like, Sleeping Beauty out."

"Could she be faking it?"

"What for? So she can jump out and yell 'Gotcha!'?"

"She might like that," Alex said. "Get our hopes up and then destroy them completely."

"Yeah. I guess you're right."

The oil diffuser cycle was coming to an end now, blue mist puffing out in fits and starts. Finally, it stopped altogether.

Alex reached out, feeling for the nearest wall. It was gone.

"What now?" he whispered.

"Grab her keys, just like we planned. But fast! Who knows how long she'll be asleep?"

Natacha was wearing a dark silk shirt and black pants. There was an odd-shaped lump in her left pocket, partially wedged between the chair and Natacha's thigh. *The bonekeys,* Alex thought. Unfortunately, they weren't within easy reach. It would require some digging to pull them out.

"Me or you?" Alex asked.

"Me," Yasmin said.

She didn't explain why, and she didn't need to. Yasmin was nimble. Alex was not. It made sense.

"Be careful," Alex said.

Yasmin took a deep breath and stretched her fingers like a pianist before a recital. She crept forward and knelt on the floor, and then, after a moment's hesitation, slid her index finger and thumb into Natacha's pocket. As Yasmin dug deeper, Alex watched the witch's face carefully for any sign that she was about to wake up. For now, at least, her snoring continued unabated.

"I feel them," Yasmin whispered. "Barely. With my fingertips." She tried to get a good grip, changing positions several times. "Ugh! I can't get ahold of them. The keys are squished against this stupid chair."

"Why don't I move her a little bit?" Alex asked.

"You sure that's a good idea?"

"Nope."

Alex stepped forward and placed his hands just behind Natacha's shoulders, locking his elbows to maintain as much distance from the witch as possible. Still, it was a lot closer than he had ever wanted to get. Her hair smelled of smoke and a sweet, fruity shampoo, like something a child might use. Looking away, Alex planted his feet and twisted his hips, aiming to turn Natacha's body just enough for Yasmin to grab the keys. He forgot to support the witch's head, however, and it fell to the side, striking the wooden frame of the chair with a loud *thunk*.

She stopped snoring.

Alex froze in horror. He wanted to let go of Natacha—*get away, get away!*—but he was afraid that the slightest movement might wake her. He remained still, watching her face, waiting for her eyes to open.

A lifetime later, wet, ragged snores filled the living room. Alex thought it was the most beautiful sound that he had ever heard.

Yasmin went back to work, and in one unexpected rush of movement, the keys slid free.

"Score," she said, raising them in triumph.

Alex carefully released Natacha's shoulders and wiped his sweaty palms on his pants. He knew he should be excited, but the mystery of how Natacha fell asleep was still nagging at him. It didn't make any sense.

Unless . . .

Alex got down on his belly and reached beneath the footstool, finding nothing but empty space. He crawled forward, tapping the wooden floor around the chair.

"Have you gone crazy?" Yasmin asked. "Let's go! We have the bonekeys!"

"One more second."

He checked behind the chair, and that's where he found her: a warm, invisible body covered with soft fur.

"It's Lenore," Alex said.

Yasmin crawled over to join him, carefully lowering her hand until she felt the cat as well.

"What's she doing here?" Yasmin asked.

"Lenore must have been in the kitchen with us," Alex said. "She heard we were in trouble, so she took the vial of sleeping oil. Then she hid here, behind the chair. When Natacha turned the diffuser on, Lenore was behind the magic walls."

"And then she poured the sleeping oil in the machine while you were reading your story," Yasmin said, nodding. "Natacha was distracted. She wouldn't have noticed an invisible cat."

Alex felt Lenore's chest, rising and falling in a steady rhythm. "But of course Lenore inhaled the sleeping oil too," he said. "She was as trapped as Natacha."

"That was so brave," Yasmin said. "Our little hero." She looked up at Alex. "We can't leave her here."

"Of course not."

He slipped his hands beneath the cat and slowly got to his feet. It was harder than he wanted to admit. Lenore was heavy to begin with, and Alex's subpar diet since becoming Natacha's prisoner had sapped his strength.

"You okay?" Yasmin asked.

"I'm fine," he said, keeping his eyes on Natacha. "But we have no idea how long this spell is going to last. Let's get out of here while we still can."

"I just have to grab our stuff first."

"We have stuff?"

Ignoring his question, Yasmin opened the closet door and dug out Alex's backpack. She had patched the hole in the bottom with duct tape.

"Food, water, coats," she said, slinging the backpack over her shoulder. "You said you saw *trees*, Alex. That doesn't sound like Flushing. The last thing we want to do is make it this far and then die in a giant forest."

"Good point," he said.

They ran down the hallway to Natacha's bedroom door. Yasmin picked through the bonekeys on the ring. The one she settled on was yellow and brittle. It looked older than the others.

It's not going to work, Alex thought as she slid the key into the crescent-shaped hole. *There's going to be another spell at play, like the one that turns the front door into a wall, and we'll find out that only Natacha can . . .*

The key turned.

Yasmin released the breath she had been holding and opened the door.

18

THE OTHER SIDE

Alex stepped over the threshold and into a forest that stretched out in every direction. Tall pine trees seemed to touch the night sky. He instantly felt woozy. The amount of open space was overwhelming, like a burst of oxygen after holding your breath for a long time.

"We're outside," he said in disbelief.

Yasmin shuffled past him, gazing up at the sky in open-mouthed wonder. Suddenly, she fell to her knees. There were tears flowing from her eyes.

"I can't believe it," she said. "After all this time . . . I never thought I would see trees again."

"Same here," Alex said. He wiped a stray tear from his own eye. "Yasmin?"

She looked up.

"Can you lock the door, please?" he asked.

With a startled gasp, Yasmin stumbled to the doorframe that sat in the center of the clearing. From the sides and back, it didn't look special at all—just three wooden beams nailed together in a rectangular shape. It was only by looking through the frame dead-on that one was able to see the hallway of the apartment.

Yasmin closed the door and turned the bonekey. The lock clicked into place.

"Do you really think that's going to keep her out?" she asked.

"I hope so," Alex said. "Those keys seem pretty one-of-a-kind. But who knows? Maybe Natacha has an extra set somewhere."

"Let's make sure we're long gone by then," Yasmin said.

Alex looked around. The trees that surrounded them were packed closely together except for a small gap directly across from the door. A path led into the deeper darkness.

"Guess we're going that way," he said.

They left the clearing and passed between the trees. There were no stars in the sky, making it difficult to see. The twisting trail was just wide enough for the two of them to walk side by side, their footsteps muffled by pine needles.

"Why isn't it cold out?" Yasmin asked.

The forest, especially at night, should have been freezing this time of year—yet the air was warm and balmy, without a single breeze to stir the trees.

"We passed through a magic portal," Alex said. "We could be anywhere in the world right now. Some place warm."

But Yasmin didn't seem to be listening to him. Her attention was elsewhere.

"That's widow grub," she said, pointing to a yellow fungus growing at the base of a tree. It glowed gently, providing a little light for them to see. "And look over there, that patch of purple flowers? Sunken lily. Sure, we could be any place on earth, but what kind of forest has magical plants?"

"This must be where Natacha gets her ingredients," Alex said.

"You didn't answer my question."

"I don't know," he said. "All we can do is keep—"

A branch snapped, cutting through the eerie silence of the forest like a gunshot.

"What was that?" Yasmin whispered. "Do you think Natacha's awake already?"

Alex shook his head.

"That didn't come from the direction of the door," he said. "It's probably just an animal or something."

"What kind of animal?"

They heard a second branch snap, a third. And then, as if some sort of gate had been lifted, an avalanche of sounds: rustling, clicking, the clap of approaching footsteps.

It wasn't just one animal. It was an entire herd. And it was heading in their direction.

The children ran.

Alex heard movement to his left and saw an odd-shaped pair of red eyes following him from between the trees. They bobbed up and down, as though the owner of the eyes was galloping. *A horse?* Alex thought. He turned his head to get a closer look and nearly lost his balance.

Just keep moving, he thought, focusing on the trail.

Carrying Lenore was starting to take its toll. His legs were weak and rubbery, his heart an angry prisoner drumming fists against its cage. More creatures joined the ones hunting them, their hoofbeats rising to a deafening crescendo. It was like being trapped in the middle of a stampede.

They're so close, he wondered. *Why don't they attack?*

He tripped.

As he fell, Alex used his arms to cushion Lenore and landed hard on his elbows. They rang out in excruciating pain. He lay there for a few moments, tasting blood in his mouth. The creatures came to a halt around him. Alex turned his head and saw narrow white legs standing just beyond the path.

He looked up.

The thing staring down at him was cut from the fabric of nightmares. It had the body of a horse, but its black hair was missing in patches, revealing large swathes of oozing skin. One eye was the size of a coffee saucer, the other no bigger than a quarter. Both were red. The worst part, however, was the black horn that protruded from the top of its head: as sharp as any blade.

It's a unicorn. Or, at least, it used to be.

Alex's fertile mind instantly recognized that there were connections to be made here. *A girl who loves unicorns. Deformed, unicorn-type creatures.* It was too strange and specific to be a coincidence. Solving that mystery would have to wait, however; right now he needed to focus on staying alive. At least two dozen unicorns were packed together along each side of the path, like a crowd gathered at a zoo exhibit. As one, they bent their heads and speared their horns forward. Alex screamed, certain that he was about to be impaled in several places, but the sharp tips of the horns fell just short of his body.

He looked at the unicorns in bewilderment as they readied themselves for a second attack.

All they have to do is take a single step forward, Alex thought. *Why do they keep their distance?*

They jabbed again. Fell short.

Gathering his senses, Alex noticed that their horns

never crossed the clearly defined line separating the path from the forest. It was as though there was an invisible wall there.

Magic, Alex concluded.

He scooped up Lenore and got to his feet. Yasmin had stopped about ten yards ahead of him. A second pack of unicorns surrounded her, pressing as close to the trail as possible without actually setting foot on it. Yasmin turned from side to side, unsure what to do. There was a bloody gash on her arm.

"Stay on the path!" Alex exclaimed. "They can't reach you there!"

Alex took a few hesitant steps forward. The unicorns followed him by shuffling their feet to the side. Their horn jabs grew frenzied and desperate.

Yasmin waited for him until he caught up.

"What are these things?" she asked.

"Monsters," Alex said. "No time to figure it out now. As long as we stay on the path, we should be safe. Well, maybe not 'safe,' exactly. More like . . . not dead."

"Close enough," said Yasmin. "Your arms must be killing you. Let's trade."

Alex was too tired to argue. He gratefully exchanged Lenore for the backpack full of supplies. After that, they navigated the trail at a half jog, too nervous to run and risk falling. The unicorns kept pace. Every so often one of them jabbed too far and recoiled in agony as silver light sparked from its horn.

Maybe the unicorns attack anyone who comes here, Alex thought. *Including Natacha. That would explain why there's a protection spell on the path. But then why doesn't she just kill the unicorns and be done with it? That seems more Natacha's style. And what does this all have to do with Unicorn Girl?* Alex's stomach churned as a horrible thought occurred to him. *Did Natacha turn the poor girl into one of these monsters as a special punishment when she tried to escape? What about the other unicorns? Are they all prisoners too?*

Alex's head spun. By opening the door to the outside world, he had somehow found more questions than answers.

The trail narrowed. Less than a foot separated them from the unicorn horns now. Alex felt like he was walking through a cave booby-trapped with spikes.

"Still think we're in a regular old forest?" Yasmin asked, carefully placing one foot in front of the other as though walking along a tightrope.

"We're outside the apartment," Alex said. "At least that's—"

He nearly fell backward as the lead unicorn kicked its front hooves into the air and neighed. The others joined in: a shrill, sad chorus. Alex covered his ears. The unicorns spun in circles, bit one another, rammed trees with their horns.

Finally, they pranced away like deer fleeing a hunting party.

"What was *that*?" Yasmin asked.

"Something spooked them."

Yasmin looked nervously into the trees.

"I don't see anything. You think it's Natacha?"

"Lenore's not awake yet," Alex said. "That means Natacha should still be asleep, too."

"Or maybe the sleeping oil affects people and cats differently," Yasmin said. "Who knows? They don't exactly teach you this stuff in school." She exhaled with relief. "At least the monsters are gone."

"Yeah," Alex said, scanning the trees. *What could have made them react that way?* He noticed a tree in the distance whose bark had been gouged away. There was something underneath it. "Pretty weird that it's unicorns, don't you think? After what we read in the library?"

"This whole thing is weird. But yeah. We're missing something."

What is that? Alex wondered, looking closer at the tree. He cleaned his glasses on the bottom of his shirt and then, looking left and right as though crossing the street, stepped off the path to get a better look.

"Hey!" Yasmin exclaimed. "What are you doing? Those things might come back!"

He saw what lay beneath the bark. For a few moments, he couldn't breathe. A heavy gloom cloaked his heart.

Please don't be true, he thought. *Please just be my overactive imagination doing its thing.*

"Look," he said, pointing at the tree. "Do you see it?"

The shocked expression on Yasmin's face was all the confirmation he needed.

That's why it isn't cold, he thought. *That's why there aren't any stars in the sky. That's why magical plants grow here.*

Beneath the bark of the tree was a second skin: red wallpaper with a black floral pattern.

"We're still inside the apartment," Yasmin said. "We never left."

"There's no way to escape." Alex's tone was clipped and matter-of-fact, all hope scrubbed away. "We're never going to see our families again."

"Stop that," Yasmin said, taking him by the shoulders. "There has to be a reason why Natacha never let us inside this particular"—she paused, considering the trees around her—"room. There must be something special about it. Let's find out what it is."

"Our plan failed."

"You're absolutely right," Yasmin said. "But you of all people should know what we do then."

"What?"

"We revise."

Alex looked into the eyes of the girl who had become his best friend in the world. The fog around his heart began to dissipate.

"There might be another exit," he said. "We have to keep looking."

Yasmin grinned.

"That's better," she said.

They climbed upward. Alex's legs throbbed in protest. He was no longer feeling hopeless, but he was still worried.

What frightened the unicorns away? Something bigger? Scarier? Whatever it is must be close. The unicorns ran away at the bottom of this hill, so . . . what's waiting for us on the other side?

The incline grew sharper as they headed toward a peak just twenty yards away. A sheen of sweat gathered between Alex's back and the backpack. He glanced at the forest behind them and wondered if they were going in the wrong direction. *We have to find out,* he thought, swallowing his fear. *There's no turning back.* Steeling himself for a new horror that would put the unicorns to shame, Alex crossed the remaining distance to the top of the hill at a run.

In the clearing below him was a tiny house made entirely from candy.

Shortbread cookies composed the exterior walls, with the occasional row of chocolate bricks for stability. Frosting caked the roof like snow. Peppermints framed sugar-glass windows latticed with gingerbread.

Alex turned to Yasmin. He was certain her startled expression mirrored his own.

"That's the house from the fairy tale," Yasmin said. "The one with the two kids whose dad leaves them in the woods."

"Hansel and Gretel," Alex said.

"There's a witch in that one, too, isn't there? And bread crumbs. I remember bread crumbs." She knelt in the dirt and pressed her face into her hands. "But it's not real. None of this is supposed to be real."

Alex took a seat next to Yasmin. She seemed more confused than ever. But to Alex, things were finally starting to make sense.

"I think Natacha is the same witch that captured Hansel and Gretel," he said.

"That's a *story*."

"Apparently not," Alex said, assembling the pieces on the fly. "Think about it—Natacha's apartment is just like that house down there. Only instead of tempting kids with candy it uses whatever they love most. Unicorns. Scary movies. Grandmas."

"Like an update," Yasmin said, mulling it over. "A more modern version."

"Exactly," Alex said. "Natacha's been alive for a long time—this proves it. In the old days, I'm sure kids got lost in the woods all the time. But now? An apartment is a better bet if you want to catch anyone."

"How many kids has she . . . ," Yasmin started. Her face set into a look of grim determination. "We can't just escape, Alex. We have to stop her."

Alex nodded.

"Let's take a closer look," he said.

"Who knows?" asked Yasmin, straightening her cap. "Maybe we'll see Snow White. Or Rapunzel. At this point, nothing will surprise me."

They followed a jelly-bean-graveled path to the front door, a slab of white chocolate panels stuck together with some kind of jam. The smell was overwhelming, a storm of sweetness that bombarded Alex's mind with delicious memories: licking chocolate batter straight from the bowl, biting into that first piece of candy at Halloween, ice cream melting on his tongue. His stomach grumbled; Alex had never been so hungry in his life. *Another trick,* he thought, tottering on his feet as the sweets beckoned him like a physical force. Alex hesitated with his hand over the doorknob; it looked like one of those button candies that you eat off long sheets of wax paper. He longed to taste it.

"Something's wrong," he said. "I think we better get out of here."

Yasmin didn't respond. He turned around and saw her shoveling giant marshmallows into her mouth.

"I'm sorry," she said. "So hungry. I can't stop . . . I can't . . ."

She collapsed onto the ground. Marshmallows rolled out of her outstretched hand.

"Yasmin!" Alex exclaimed, only the words sounded funny to him. Garbled. And then he realized: *My mouth is full.* He tasted something blissfully sweet and saw the candy doorknob in his hand. Or rather, half the candy doorknob.

I don't even remember taking a bite, he thought, still chewing. A soothing warmth spread throughout his body. He fell.

19

NATACHA'S STORY

The entire world was shaking.

Alex groggily opened his eyes. He heard rattling glass, felt something solid vibrating beneath his head. He tried to remember where he was. *Candy house,* he thought, the gears of his brain beginning to spin again. *I ate . . . a doorknob? Why did I eat a doorknob?*

The world blurred into focus.

He was on the floor of a kitchen. It looked like something you might see during a field trip to a historical village: stone floor and walls, long benches beneath a simple wooden table. Across from him was a massive iron door. It was partially open, revealing a deep recess filled with charred wood.

I'm inside the candy house, Alex thought. *That's the oven from the fairy tale, where the witch . . .*

Terror slapped him awake. He pushed himself into a sitting position. As he did, the room finally stopped shaking.

Behind him: a chopping noise.

Alex straightened his glasses and turned around. Natacha was standing on the other side of the room. She wasn't facing him, but he could see the butcher's knife in her hand. She raised and lowered it with violent enthusiasm, hacking away at something on the wooden counter in front of her.

"Finally," Natacha said without turning around. "It's been almost two days. I thought you were never going to wake up. Even after all these years, the magic in that candy still packs a wallop. Lures kids into eating it whether they want to or not, and then—there's little else to do but wait. You know how powerful sleeping spells can be. Don't you, Alex?"

To Natacha's left, a cauldron hung from an iron hook. Steam rose from its surface, courtesy of the flickering flames beneath it. The spicy smell of stew filled the room.

"Where's Yasmin?" he asked.

"Alive," Natacha said. "For now. Provided you help me."

"Help you with what?"

Natacha flung a handful of something red and stringy into the cauldron. It made a sizzling noise as it hit the broth.

"You felt the house rumble," Natacha said. "Third time

this hour. It's getting worse. She needs a story, Alex. I tried reading her one of the old ones from the library. It doesn't work anymore. She only wants *yours*."

"What do you mean, *she*?" Alex asked. "I thought you said the stories were for the apartment."

Natacha slammed the knife down.

"She *is* the apartment, Alex. Don't you understand anything? They're one and the same now!"

Natacha turned around. Her face was haggard and drawn, her eyes sunk deep in their sockets.

"Would you like to hear a story?" she asked.

Alex nodded and pulled himself onto a bench at the kitchen table. Things were still fuzzy, and the longer Natacha talked, the more time he had to clear his head. He would have to be at his best to rescue Yasmin.

The stew popped and bubbled.

"How old do you think I am?" Natacha asked.

Alex considered the question—*What should I admit I know?* He decided that the time for deceit had passed.

"In your hundreds," Alex said.

"I'm twenty-nine."

"You *look* twenty-nine," Alex corrected her. "But you've been alive for—"

"Twenty-nine years," Natacha said. "Almost thirty. I was going to give you a slice of my birthday cake in a few weeks. I don't see that happening now."

"That can't be right," Alex said, shaking his head. "The blue mist . . ."

"Ah," said Natacha, amused. "You thought it was—what? Some kind of immortality oil? Doesn't exist."

"The blue mist isn't magic?"

"Oh, it's magic, all right. Just not the kind you're thinking of. We'll get to that later. Let me start from the beginning." She stirred the stew with a long wooden ladle. "When I was a little younger than you, about twenty years ago, Aunt Gris took me prisoner."

"The . . . who?" Alex asked, baffled. "Took *you* prisoner? What are you talking about?"

"Her full name was Griselda," Natacha said, snapping the syllables with her tongue. "But she insisted that we call her Aunt Gris. She was the original witch who lived in the apartment. For all I know, she might be the original *witch*, period. She created all this. The candy house. The forest. The magic rooms." Natacha smiled slightly. "You'll never believe how she tricked me into crossing the threshold. I was *obsessed* with unicorns at the time, and I—"

"—followed one inside the apartment building," Alex said, the words spilling from his stunned lips.

Natacha stopped stirring.

"How did you know that?" she asked.

"You're Unicorn Girl!" Alex exclaimed, dizzy with revelation.

"What?"

"You never wrote your name," he added, "so that's what we called you. We read what you wrote inside the storybooks when you were a girl."

Natacha straightened, the gears of her memory starting to turn.

"I *did* write in the storybooks, didn't I?" she asked. "It seems so long ago, another life. That's how you knew about the sleeping oil, isn't it?"

Alex nodded.

"Only—I never wrote down the final ingredient, so how . . ." Natacha looked abashed, like a student who finally figures out an answer that should have been obvious from the start. "That story about the baker's daughter! You tricked me into telling you!"

"Yes," Alex said.

Natacha looked at him with something approaching respect.

"You're smarter than you look, storyteller," she said.

Alex disagreed. If he was that intelligent, he would have figured out Natacha's true identity long ago. As it was, his understanding of past events had been completely shattered, making him wonder what else he had gotten wrong. He felt like he had been reading the pages of a story in the wrong order.

"Aunt Gris," Alex said, pushing his glasses back. "You

don't mean to say that she's the witch from 'Hansel and Gretel,' do you? That's just a story. It never really happened."

"Says the boy sitting in a house made of candy," Natacha replied, raising her eyebrows. "I don't know who came first, the witch or the story. In any case, *she's* the one who's been alive forever. It wasn't any oils or potions that did it, though. No—the magic Aunt Gris used was far older than that. She ate children and devoured their youth."

Natacha's eyes looked past him at the massive oven built into the wall. Alex took a quick glance and turned away, his imagination blasting him with unwanted images. *I used to love the witch in "Hansel and Gretel,"* he thought. *The way she tried to fatten Hansel up so there would be more of him to cook—so creepy.*

That was before he knew she was real.

"I wasn't the only one she captured," Natacha said, staring at the oven with great intensity. "There was a boy a few years older than me. Ian. He watched out for me, taught me what I needed to do to stay safe, until Aunt Gris started to grow old again and needed to replenish her lost youth." Natacha scrubbed her hands together as though washing them beneath running water. "She made me clean the oven afterward. Closed the door behind me until it was all spic-and-span. I was in there for hours, in the dark. That was the day I decided that I was never going to be powerless again."

Alex felt a chill run up his spine. *Unicorn Girl climbed into the oven that day,* he thought, *and someone completely different climbed out.* It made him sad.

"I waited for my opportunity," Natacha said. "I read Aunt Gris her nightly tale and played the faithful little servant. The library, if you haven't guessed by now, belonged to her. She's the one obsessed with scary stories." Natacha's expression grew sly. "But I pretended to love them, just like her, and in time Aunt Gris grew to trust me. One day she took me through her secret door, to this very kitchen, and told me how the apartment was just a facade to trick children. The true house is the one we're sitting in right now. It's the beating heart, the source of all the magic."

Natacha ladled stew into two clay bowls. She slid one across the table and took a seat.

"She taught me a few potions, too," Natacha continued. "Nothing complicated. Nothing that she ever imagined I could use against her. But she underestimated my gift for such things, and one night—we were here in the candy house, just before story time—I slipped a sleeping potion into her tea. She fell to the floor, and I listened, ever so carefully, until her breathing became slow and steady. Then I raised my knife into the air. . . ." She glanced at Alex's stew. "You're not eating."

"What?" he asked, as though awoken from a dream. "I'm not hungry."

"Are you sure?" Natacha stirred her stew with a wooden spoon. Steam rose in undulating waves. "I made it special. Just for you."

Alex stared down at his bowl with a growing sense of dismay. He had never smelled stew like this before. He poked it with his spoon. Chunks of white meat bobbed to the surface.

A horrible thought slithered into his mind.

"Where's Lenore?" he asked quietly.

"Lenore?" Natacha asked, lingering on the word as though it were a name she hadn't heard in years. "You mean, the useless beast who betrayed me?" She took a healthy bite of the stew and chewed thoughtfully. "Don't worry about her."

Alex stared down at his stew, fighting the nausea rising up his throat.

She couldn't have, he thought. *That's too horrible, even for her.*

"Wait!" Natacha exclaimed, choking back laughter. "Did you think . . . I *cooked* the cat?"

"Didn't you?" Alex asked.

Natacha exploded with laughter. She pounded the table, guffawing uncontrollably.

"Why in the world would I ruin a perfectly good stew?"

she asked. "You know how *old* that cat is? She's probably all string and gristle inside."

Unsure what to believe, Alex reexamined the stew in front of him. *I guess that* could *be chicken,* he thought. *And as for the strange smell—who knows what weird spices she threw in there?*

"At first I was mad you tried to escape," Natacha said. "And I won't lie, I considered some pretty horrific punishments—but then I remembered that I had done the exact same thing when I was your age! Which got me thinking—maybe things could be different between us. That's why I'm telling you my story, Alex. You're a child of darkness, just like me. You don't need to return to a world that doesn't understand. You can make a home here, as I have. Not as my captive. As a friend."

Alex stared at Natacha in utter disbelief. *I'm nothing like you!* he started to scream. *You've hurt people! How can I ever be your friend?* But then he saw Natacha's downcast eyes and the nervous way she plucked at the tiny hairs on her arm, and a shocking realization kept him from speaking.

She's lonely, he thought.

It was strange to imagine that Natacha might desire human companionship just like anyone else, but he supposed it made sense. She had been alone in the apartment for two decades. He had no desire to be her friend, of course, but he couldn't just turn her down. She would be furious, and then Alex wouldn't be able to help Yasmin and Lenore at all.

I have to go along with it for now, he thought. *Put her at ease.*

"I didn't want to admit it at first," Alex said, managing a small smile. "But in a strange way, I do feel at home here."

"I knew it!" Natacha exclaimed, throwing her arms into the air. She seemed so genuinely thrilled that Alex almost felt guilty for lying to her. "You won't regret this, Alex! Of course you're going to have to work your way back into my trust, but after that things are—"

The house trembled. Stew spilled down the swinging cauldron and spattered into the flames. The disturbance only lasted a few seconds, but it was long enough to apply a fresh coat of worry to Natacha's face.

"We can't wait any longer," she said, sliding off the bench. "You have to tell her a story. Something she's never heard before."

"Why do you keep saying 'she'?" Alex asked.

Natacha smiled with wicked delight and she wrapped her arm around his shoulder.

"Forget all about your ghosts and goblins and vampires," she said. "I'm going to show you something *really* scary."

20

AUNT GRIS

Natacha led him along a dank corridor and into a circular chamber. There was a coffin at its center. It was made from a blue, crystalline material—*rock candy,* Alex thought—and suspended from the ceiling by black licorice. To its left sat a silver machine, similar to Natacha's oil diffuser but much larger. A long plastic tube connected the machine to a nozzle in the bottom of the coffin. Red mist swirled through the tube, clouding the crystalline walls of the coffin and obscuring its interior.

"Alex!" shouted a familiar voice.

He spun around. Iron gates were evenly spaced around the stone wall like the numbers of a clock. Behind them he could see tiny cells. *This must be where Aunt Gris kept her captives, back in the fairy-tale days,* he thought. Yasmin was in a cell on the opposite side of the chamber, her face pressed against the bars. At some point she had lost her cap. As Yasmin brushed the hair from her eyes, Lenore peeked out from between her legs and regarded Alex like a child arriving late to class: *Where have you been?*

"Alex?" Yasmin asked. She took in the situation with a perplexed expression: Why was he standing beside Natacha and making no attempt to help her? "Are you under a spell?"

"Quiet, girl," Natacha said. "The storyteller is no longer your friend. He's with me now. Isn't that right?"

Natacha stared hard at Alex, daring him to contradict her.

"That's right," he said. "Sorry, Yasmin. This is who I really am."

He saw the betrayal in Yasmin's eyes and quickly turned away, his heart aching. Natacha nodded with approval and led him to the coffin.

"Meet the great and powerful Aunt Gris," she said, running her hand along the jagged coffin lid. "Before I could bring the knife down and finish what I started, the house sealed her inside this . . . shell. It was protecting itself, you see. When a witch dies, all of her magic is undone. The house and everything connected to it would fall apart."

"The house is alive?" Alex asked.

"It can't talk or anything like that," Natacha said. "But it's like you and me, Alex. It knows how to survive. It connected itself to the witch, sapped her magic. This way it could offer me a reason to keep her alive."

Natacha snapped a shard off the coffin lid and held it before her eyes. Light prismed through its craggy surface and cast her face in a sickly blue glow.

"It's made of candy, you know," she said. "The first time I saw it, I couldn't resist taking a tiny nibble, just to see what would happen. That was a mistake. I was sick for weeks. But the power it gave me, the things I could do . . ." Her eyes glowed with remembrance. "I cast my first spell by mistake. I held my unicorn pendant in my hand and wished it was real—and there they were! I created *life*! Isn't that magnificent?"

Alex nodded eagerly, concealing his real reaction: *Those things you created are monsters, not unicorns.*

"After that, there was no going back," Natacha said. "I learned that just a tiny piece of the coffin, like the one in my hand here, could be boiled down to its essence and turned into an entire vat of oil that lasted for months. All I had to do was breathe it in for a few minutes each day, and Aunt Gris's magic could be mine."

That's what the blue mist was for, Alex thought. *Natacha's daily intake of magic.*

"You were free," Alex said. "Why didn't you leave the apartment? Go back to your family?"

"And been what?" Natacha snapped. "Just a normal

girl again? I don't think so."

"You could have been a good witch," Alex said. "You didn't have to hurt any of those kids."

"That's not *my* fault!" Natacha exclaimed. "The apartment brought them to my door. I set the first few free, but . . . I was punished. For a long time, the magic oil didn't work anymore. What choice did I have?"

You could have stopped, Alex thought. *You could have done the right thing.*

But that would have meant giving up magic, and for Natacha that was no option at all. In some ways, she had never stopped being the apartment's prisoner.

Biting back his fear, Alex bent down and peered through the side of the coffin. A red scrim covered its sides like algae on the glass of a fish tank. He could just barely glimpse a figure inside. It had a vaguely human shape, but the dimensions were all off.

"What's wrong with her?" Alex asked.

"Aunt Gris has been in there a long time," Natacha said. "She's as much a part of the house now as . . . There were bound to be certain changes. It doesn't matter. The important thing is that she stays asleep. And that's where you come in, my friend. The sleeping oil doesn't work as well as it used to. Aunt Gris gets restless. You've seen what happens."

"The earthquakes," Alex said.

"Exactly," Natacha said. "The only thing that can put her back to sleep again are scary stories. They calm her down, like lullabies soothe a baby. Maybe they give her beautiful nightmares." She grinned as an idea struck her. "You should try it! The oil. Once you see what it's like to have magic at your fingertips"—she clapped her hands, suddenly as giddy as a child—"I could teach you how to cast spells! Think about it, Alex. Wouldn't *being* a warlock be a lot better than writing about one?"

The strained smile on Natacha's face did little to hide her desperation. Alex felt an inkling of pity.

"If I stay," he said, "will you let Yasmin and Lenore go?"

"Of course," Natacha said. "No harm will come to them."

Alex smiled with relief, as though Natacha had set his mind at rest. He knew she was lying, though.

As soon as he told his story, he'd never see his friends again.

Without warning, the entire room jerked to the left like a carnival ride. Iron gates squealed against their moorings. Cots flew across their cells. A misshapen chunk of the coffin lid plummeted to the floor and shattered like a glass vase. With a shout of anguish, Natacha fell to her knees and frantically gathered the pieces.

"Tell a story!" she exclaimed. "Quick!"

"I don't have one!"

"Just make it up!"

"It's not that easy."

"Then tell her a true story," Natacha said. "The reason you wanted to destroy your nightbooks! She'll like that."

"That's not scary."

"It was to you," Natacha said. "Something made you terrified of your own stories, of the kind of person who could have such dreadful ideas. Feed her your fear!"

The magical quake rose in intensity. A crack appeared in the stone wall. The coffin swung back and forth like a vampire's hammock. Alex remained silent. *All I have to do is keep my mouth shut,* he thought, *and Aunt Gris will eventually wake up.* He didn't like the idea of bringing another evil witch into the world. But at least it was an evil witch who probably hated Natacha even more than they did.

"Why aren't you starting?" Natacha asked.

Alex clenched his lips together and stared back at her with defiance.

"Fine," Natacha said, raising her hands into the air. They thrummed with gathering power. "Let me make this easy. You either tell your story right now or I will turn the girl to dust and make you sweep her up!"

Alex looked at the coffin. There was no movement. No sign that Aunt Gris was going to wake up in the next minute or two. If he tried to wait it out, Natacha would have plenty of time to hurt his friends.

But what if there was a way I could force her to wake up? he wondered, formulating a plan.

"Last chance!" Natacha said, raising her hands higher.

"Okay," Alex said. "I'll do it."

He turned toward the coffin. There was no need to speak loudly. Aunt Gris was part of the house. If she could hear him when he read stories in the living room, she could certainly hear him when he was standing three feet away.

Alex took a big breath. *Just like Scheherazade on the one-thousand-and-first night,* he thought.

"I was in math," he said, "when my teacher got a call from the office and said that Mr. Calkins wanted to see me. I went, 'Who's Mr. Calkins?' because I really had no idea, and Greg Jenkins said, 'He's the guy who talks to the crazy kids.' The class thought that was pretty funny. I left quick. It took me a while to find Mr. Calkins's office, and when I finally did I guess he'd been waiting a while, because he looked pretty annoyed. 'Mosher, right?' he asked, consulting this file on his desk. 'Alexander?' I nodded even though no one ever calls me Alexander. I sat down and he closed the door behind us."

The walls of the room began to shake a little less, like an audience quieting down as a performance begins.

"Mr. Calkins asked me a bunch of questions. 'How's school?' and 'How are things at home?' Icebreakers. I answered him as best I could, but in my head I'm trying to figure out what I'm doing there. I'm not a troublemaker. I'm not flunking out of school. I'm no one. And then Mr. Calkins lifted the file with my name on it and I saw how thick it was, just stuffed with papers, and he said, 'I've been looking through some of your writing through the years. Your teachers photocopied the more disturbing stories. Did you know that?' I didn't know that. I thought my teachers always liked me."

With a final shudder, like a train car coming to rest at a station, the rumbling came to a complete stop. Natacha, grinning from ear to ear, circled her hand in a clockwise motion: *Keep going, keep going!*

"Mr. Calkins is a gum chewer," Alex said, back in the office now, reliving every moment. "He pops one in his mouth and offers me a piece. I take it but just hold it in my hand. He asks me if I have bad thoughts. Nightmares. Do I play first-person shooters? Watch violent movies? Do I imagine the gruesome things I write about happening to real people? My family? Kids at school? I shake my head. I tell him that the stories don't mean anything. They're just make-believe. Mr. Calkins nods and makes a note in my file. He thinks I'm lying. I can tell. He thinks there's something wrong with me. And who am I to argue? He has degrees on his wall. He wears a tie. He's an expert." Alex cleared his parched throat; it felt like it was coated with sand. "I decided right there and then to destroy my nightbooks and never write another scary story again. I was terrified that if I didn't stop, I would end up being the boy that Mr. Calkins already imagined me to be."

Natacha's applause echoed through the silent room.

"Perfect!" she exclaimed. "The pain in your voice—the *fear*! Bravo! She is going to sleep like a baby!"

"I'm not done," Alex said.

Natacha froze, unsure what to make of this unexpected development. Alex didn't give her a chance to think too long. He jumped right into the next part of his story.

"Instead of destroying my nightbooks," he said, "I was captured by a witch. She said there was darkness in my heart. I wondered if she was right, especially after what happened with Mr. Calkins. Maybe this was meant to be. But I quickly discovered that real darkness isn't fun, like in stories. People die. You can't click the backspace key and bring them back to life again. I hated it. It's not who I am at all."

The room started to rumble again. *It's working,* Alex thought with relief. Until this point he hadn't been sure if his theory was correct.

"What are you doing?" Natacha asked, a warning tone in her voice.

Alex ignored her.

"And now I realize—so what if I write scary stories? I might hurt someone with nouns and adjectives, but I would never hurt someone for real. In fact, I think I might be kind of brave! I wouldn't go as far as heroic—that would be pushing it—but the next time John calls me a scaredy-cat, I'm going to tell him about the time I squashed a dangler beneath my foot or escaped a forest of scary unicorns. He won't believe how tough his little brother was! He'll be proud of me!"

Inside the coffin, Aunt Gris shifted.

If scary stories are the sweet dreams that lull her to sleep, Alex thought, backing toward the other side of the room, *then courage, friendship, compassion—those are the nightmares that will wake her up.*

Alex just hoped he had enough time to finish the job. Natacha was onto him. She strode across the floor, her hands outstretched in a threatening manner, but the room trembled—a solid eight on the Richter scale this time around—and the witch fell backward.

A chunk of the ceiling crashed to the floor and obliterated the oil diffuser. Red mist leaked from the hole in the bottom of the coffin.

"No!" Natacha screamed, forgetting about Alex for a moment. She scrambled to the coffin, intent on finding a way to plug the leak.

"Maybe I wouldn't have been so brave if I was alone,"

Alex continued, smiling at Yasmin, "but I met an extraordinary girl who's smart and loyal and brave, and a cat willing to risk her life for her friends. They gave me courage. And the stories I was so worried about? They saved my life! Why did I want to destroy them? It seems so ridiculous now! There's nothing wrong with me. I'm not bad. I'm not weird. I'm just a kid who likes monsters!"

He checked on Natacha. She had given up trying to chase him. Instead, she was pulling strands of crimson light from several invisible pockets in the air and tying them into a complicated knot. The expression on her face had moved beyond anger into an all-encompassing rage.

"So no matter what happens," Alex said, knowing that he had only seconds to spare, "I'm glad I was sent to Mr. Calkins's office that day. I'm grateful for my time in apartment 4E. If I had never come here, I would still be the same old Alex Mosher, too scared and embarrassed to be who I am. My story might have started out on a sour note, but it has a happy ending!"

The light between Natacha's hands, a blinding sun now, promised a fate far worse than being turned into a porcelain figurine. She raised it above her head.

"Good-bye, storyteller," she said.

With an ear-shattering *whoosh*, the coffin lid rocketed from its perch and landed on the other side of the room. It shattered into a million pieces. Shards of rock candy stung

Alex's face like a hailstorm.

He hardly noticed. He was too intent on the center of the room.

From inside the coffin, a hand rose into the air.

Its fingers were candy canes ending in chiseled nails that looked very, very sharp. They twisted and cracked, testing their newfound freedom. A second hand, much like the first, gripped the side of the coffin.

Aunt Gris pushed herself up.

You could tell that she had been human at one point. Her ears and nose were in the expected places, but her face drooped like melted taffy, and her eyes were gold-foiled chocolate coins pressed deeply into malleable flesh.

Alex didn't scream. He tried to, but there was suddenly no air left in his lungs. He felt like someone had hit him in the stomach with a baseball bat.

What have I done?

Aunt Gris fixed her eyes on Natacha. The witch dropped the ball of light in her hands like a child caught with a forbidden treat. It vanished.

"You're awake!" Natacha said, pasting an unconvincing smile on her face. "At last! I've been trying to undo the terrible curse on you for ages!"

The thing that used to be Aunt Gris gave no acknowledgment that she heard—or understood—the words. She stared at her candy-cane fingers in astonishment, as though seeing them for the first time. Her fingers crackled as she opened and closed her hands.

"The house used its magic to keep you alive," Natacha said. "There were some . . . unfortunate side effects."

Aunt Gris lifted herself out of the coffin and stepped onto the floor, tottering unsteadily before rising to her full height. She was wearing a flowing burgundy dress with lots of ruffles. Her body was grotesquely tall and thin, as though it had been stretched along with her face.

"Alex," Yasmin whispered. "The keys are hanging from the wall! Let us out."

It was as good a time as any. Both witches were distracted: Aunt Gris trying to figure out how to maneuver her new body, Natacha playing the role of dutiful servant. "Good, good," she said, holding Aunt Gris's elongated fingers as though she were a child learning how to skate. "Just like that. Left, right. Left, right."

Alex retrieved the keys and opened the cell door as quietly as possible. The children crept toward the exit to the chamber, Lenore just behind them.

"Don't worry," Natacha said. "You'll be right as rain in no time at all. You need sustenance—life force to replace all that you've lost." She moved to the side, allowing Aunt Gris a clear view of Alex and Yasmin. "That's why I brought these two! I know you prefer them cooked, but I think in this case you can make an exception."

Aunt Gris, upon seeing the children, shuddered with anticipation. Her gold-foiled eyes jumped between Alex and Yasmin, like a starving diner trying to choose between two equally delicious desserts. She took a single step forward . . . and then stopped.

Aunt Gris pointed a candy-caned finger in Natacha's direction.

"I remember now," she said in a guttural voice that seemed to claw its way out of her throat. "You're the one who put me to sleep! You're the one who changed me into this *thing*."

For a moment, Natacha looked ready to deny it, to tell any lie in order to save her life. Then her face hardened into a defiant expression.

"Yes," she snapped. "It *was* me. What are you going to do about it? I'm not a weak little girl anymore. I'm a witch!"

She raised her right hand and a spear of black ice shot from her palm. Aunt Gris swatted it away like a bothersome fly. Natacha snarled with frustration and unleashed a barrage of spells, one after the other: choking mist, nooses made of flame, twin skeletons brandishing iron swords. Alex knew they should run, but he couldn't turn away. It was an awe-inspiring display of magic.

Aunt Gris was not as impressed. She turned each spell away without any effort.

Finally, Natacha raised her hands and nothing happened at all. She fell to her knees.

"Oh dear," Aunt Gris said. "It looks like you've run out of magic." She smiled, revealing peppermint-bark fangs and a forked tongue of braided licorice. "Fortunately, I don't have that problem. I'm a *real* witch. But you? You're nothing but a little *thief*!"

Natacha tried to run. She didn't get far. Aunt Gris leaped across the room and landed on her back. Yasmin and Alex didn't wait to see what happened next. They ran. Behind them, they heard a short scream of pain followed by horrible crunching sounds—and then nothing at all.

21

UNEXPECTED MAGIC

They burst out of the house and into the dark forest. Yasmin was a lot faster than Alex, her arms pumping like the pistons of a steam engine. Nevertheless, Alex was able to keep up. Every time he fell behind, he just imagined what would happen if Aunt Gris caught him. It was a powerful motivator.

"What are we . . . going to do?" Alex asked between deep gasps of air. "Even if . . . we make it . . . back to the apartment, we're . . . still trapped!"

"Lenore and I have it covered," Yasmin said. "Save your breath for running."

They reached the bottom of the hill. The unicorns paced them on either side, jabbing their horns at the children. Alex tried to stay on the path, but it was hard to do while running. He felt a horn scratch his shoulder, his calf.

Yasmin slapped a hand to her side and screamed in pain.

Why are the unicorns still here? Alex thought. *Natacha said that when a witch dies, all her magic is undone.* But then he realized that it hadn't truly been Natacha who created the unicorns. She had stolen the magic from Aunt Gris.

Behind them, they heard a voice that echoed magically throughout the entire forest.

"Children?" Aunt Gris said. "Are you *hiding* from me? How delightful!"

Alex ran faster, regretting, for the first time, his life-long hatred of exercise. His heart felt like it was going to explode. The air in his lungs thinned to a trickle.

He ignored it all.

RUN!

Finally, they reached the door to the apartment.

There was no longer any need for the bonekeys. The door had been blown from the frame. Charred splinters crunched beneath Alex's shoes.

Natacha blasted it off with magic, he thought. *Guess she didn't have an extra set of keys after all.*

The children ran down the hallway and into the living room. Alex's heart fell. The wall that blocked their passage to the outside world seemed more impassable than ever.

"Okay, Lenore," Yasmin said. "Do your thing."

"What thing?" Alex asked. The beating of his heart sounded like a metronome turned to its highest setting.

He leaned on a table, afraid he was going to collapse, and saw his nightbook sitting there. An idea stirred.

If only we can get out of here . . .

"Lenore got a full dose of the sleeping oil," Yasmin said. "But that wasn't all. She breathed in the mist that gave Natacha her magic, too. So I figure . . . she's got a few spells in her."

"She's a cat."

Lenore puffed out her chest: *Exactly.* She raised a single paw into the air and closed her eyes in concentration. Nothing happened.

"Give her a chance," Yasmin said with a nervous smile. "We tried it out in the cell. She made a spoon float in the air."

This is a little different, Alex thought, but he didn't want to be discouraging. He looked down the hallway and into the forest. It remained empty.

For now.

"You almost had it!" Yasmin exclaimed with encouragement. "I definitely saw something flicker there for a moment! Keep trying, Lenore!" She turned to Alex. "Any sign of Aunt Gris?"

"Not yet," he said, glancing in her direction. Lenore was floating slightly off the ground, both paws raised now. "I'll let you know the moment—"

Aunt Gris appeared in the doorway.

"I recognize that voice," she said, entering the apartment. "The storyteller. I owe you my gratitude for the pleasant dreams you've given me these past few weeks."

"So you won't eat me?"

"On the contrary," Aunt Gris said, "it just makes me more curious what you might taste like."

She took a large bite of her index finger and crunched it between her teeth. It instantly grew back again.

"Alex!" Yasmin screamed.

The front door had not only appeared—it was open. Beyond it, Alex could see the fourth-floor hallway, drab and ugly and fantastically real.

He grabbed his nightbook and ran, gritting his teeth as he leaped across the threshold, certain that some kind of magic would hold him back. Then he heard the muffled sound of the frayed hallway rug beneath his sneakers and knew that he was free.

He grinned at Yasmin, who was running right beside him. *We're out of the apartment!* he thought triumphantly. *For real this time!*

That didn't mean they were safe, though. Alex glanced over his shoulder to see if Natacha was following them, and saw that Lenore had stopped outside the apartment door. She raised her paws in the air, casting another spell. *What's she doing?* Alex wondered, and then he saw Aunt Gris try to leap into the hallway—and crash into an invisible barrier instead.

She hissed in frustration and glared down at Lenore.

"I see Natacha is not the only one who's been stealing my magic," the witch said. "I'm disappointed, Lenore. After all those centuries we spent together, I expected more loyalty from you."

That's why Natacha never liked Lenore, Alex thought, still moving toward the elevator at the end of the hall. *She wasn't even her cat.*

Lenore looked up at Aunt Gris and meowed pleadingly.

"You've grown soft in your old age, my friend," Aunt Gris said. "I'm afraid the children really do have to die. And then I'll come back and deal with you."

The witch ran a single nail along the invisible barrier. A long scratch began to appear. Lenore turned to Alex. Her use of magic had taken its toll. She looked like she was about to collapse from exhaustion.

That's all I can do, she seemed to say. *I'm sorry.*

She vanished.

The children ran to the elevator at the end of the hall. Yasmin punched the panel. For once, the doors opened right away. Alex hurried inside and pressed the *B* button while Yasmin repeatedly jabbed the button to close the doors. Finally, they slid shut.

The elevator's gears squeaked to life. They started to descend.

"You have a plan?" Yasmin asked.

Alex raised the nightbook in his hands.

"Not exactly," he said. "More of an idea. First thing we have to do is get to the basement. After that—"

The lights went off, plunging them into darkness. Footsteps skittered across the roof of the elevator.

"She's here," Yasmin whispered.

Alex nodded, afraid to move. The elevator rocked back and forth like a ship at sea. Above them, the witch stomped her feet and giggled.

The car fell.

Alex loved thrill rides as much as the next twelve-year-old, but this wasn't like Freefall or Tower of Terror. This was horrifying. The children screamed as they plummeted to earth, the car banging against the walls of the shaft like a runaway train. Alex closed his eyes and awaited the inevitable crash.

They jerked to a sudden halt.

Yasmin and Alex fell together in a tangle of arms and legs. They quickly got to their feet, bruised but okay.

The elevator doors opened. Yasmin peeked out.

"It's the basement, just like you wanted," she said. "Yay?"

They stepped onto the concrete floor and the elevator doors instantly closed behind them. Alex heard a sizzling sound and saw the handle to the stairwell melt away.

No way to escape, he thought.

Aunt Gris cackled. It seemed everywhere at once.

"Come on," Alex whispered.

They wove between towering stacks of boxes and into an open area where larger items were stored: a rotted crib overflowing with doll parts, moldy sofas with springs busting through the cushions, and an old pinball machine with a cracked display. Alex could hear the rush of flames as Old Smokey, the ancient boiler, worked hard to keep its charges nice and toasty. He walked faster.

"Okay," Yasmin said. "What's this plan of yours?"

"We're doing it."

"Walking?"

"No," he whispered. "We're leading the witch toward the—"

Yasmin screamed as she flew backward. Alex spun around and saw his friend in Aunt Gris's outstretched hands. The witch leaned forward and opened her jaws far wider than should have been possible. She seemed determined to fit Yasmin's entire head into her mouth.

Alex opened his nightbook.

"Jason couldn't decide which was stranger," he read, "the fact that his sister died every Tuesday at eleven fifteen, or that she always came back to life twenty-two minutes later."

Aunt Gris shook her head like a student caught not paying attention in class.

"What was that?" she asked. "What did you say?"

Alex read the next line.

"Zachary didn't think his day could get any worse—until he looked out his car window and saw the monsters."

This time, Alex had truly caught the witch's attention. *She really does love scary stories,* he thought. Perhaps the sentences would have had less power if she had heard them already, but these were from failed stories that he never finished or simply threw away. He had liked their openings, however, and written them down on a single page.

Alex remembered something that Ms. Coral had once told them: *Every sentence is a learning experience—no writing is ever wasted.* He hoped he had a chance to tell her how right she was.

"The Gleaming City was a marvel of the modern world, all silver and chrome and glass, except for the ancient hole at its center."

Alex started to walk backward. Aunt Gris followed him as though in a trance, releasing Yasmin without even realizing it. Alex glanced over his shoulder, making sure that he wasn't going to trip over anything. Right now he was casting a spell of his own, and the slightest interruption might break its magic.

"As Mr. Levine wrote the math problem, a sentence scrawled itself into the blackboard just above his head. I was the only one who could see it."

Alex could feel Old Smokey's heat on his back. *Almost there,* he thought.

"Addie had always thought that clowns were the scariest part of the circus," he read. "She was wrong."

"Give me the book," Aunt Gris said. She held out her candy-caned fingers, a hungry, desperate look in her eyes. "I *need* it."

Keeping one eye on the witch, Alex cautiously opened the heavy iron door to Old Smokey. It was even larger than him.

Inside the boiler, flames roared.

"What are you doing?" Aunt Gris asked, crossing half the space between them in a heartbeat.

Alex read from his nightbook, freezing the witch in her tracks.

"When I woke up that morning, there was a package wrapped in brown paper waiting on my front porch. My address had been written in clear, crisp handwriting: Forty-Two Skybird Lane, Hennington, PA. That wasn't the strange part. The strange part was the name written above the address, which wasn't a name at all. It read: 'To the Man Standing Right Behind You.' I turned around."

Aunt Gris grinned with childlike pleasure.

"What happens next?" she asked. *"I have to know!"*

"Good," said Alex.

He threw the nightbook into the flames.

The witch screamed in horror and leaped across the floor, knocking Alex out of the way as she stuck her hands into the raging heat. "Nooooo!" she wailed, clawing desperately for the nightbook. "What have you done! The stories! *The stories!*"

Yasmin shoved her from behind.

Aunt Gris fell forward into the flames. Alex slammed the boiler door shut, and the two children held their backs against it as the witch struggled to escape. Finally, there was a sound like rice pouring into a bowl and the witch stopped struggling. The smell of burned candy apples filled the air. Alex peeked through the tiny slot in the door. There was nothing left of Aunt Gris but a large mound of sugar and four candy-cane fingers. They were still wrapped around the remains of his nightbook.

22

THE GIFT

It had been unusually hot all May, and that Saturday was no exception. By the time Yasmin finally arrived at the park, Alex's favorite Cthulhu T-shirt was stuck to his back.

"Sorry I'm late," Yasmin said, taking a seat next to him on the bench. She was holding a small paper bag in her hands. "I had to finish something up."

After a few months of home-cooked meals, the color had finally returned to Yasmin's skin. When she smiled her cheeks looked healthy and full.

"That's okay," Alex said. "I was just sitting here pondering."

"New story?"

"No," he said. "I mean—yes. I'm working on something, a novel actually. But mostly I was thinking how weird it was—my brother yelled at me this morning for something so stupid it's not even worth getting into, and I'm *ecstatic* about it. For months my family has been walking around on eggshells, being so nice to me I felt like a stranger in my own home. Now I feel like things are finally returning to normal."

"I know what you mean," Yasmin said. "The other day my mom tore into me for texting Claire when I was supposed to be doing my homework, and I could have hugged her."

Yasmin and Alex were at the center of a mystery that had captivated the entire world. Fifty-eight confused children—including Yasmin's friends Claire, Eli, and Little Hwan—had been found wandering the halls of Bayside Apartments. They recalled their names and everything about their lives up until the moment they entered apartment 4E, but nothing past that. Even more extraordinary, some of the children had been missing for a decade or more and hadn't seemed to age in the intervening years. There was talk of aliens and government conspiracies, but for the families who had finally been reunited after years of grief, there was only one explanation: miracle.

Yasmin and Alex could have shed a considerable amount of light on the subject. They might have told authorities how the missing children hadn't aged because they had been frozen as figurines. They could have also explained how the death of the witch who owned the apartment broke the curse and brought the children back to life.

Unfortunately, Yasmin and Alex didn't think anyone would believe them, especially since the apartment had reverted back to a completely nonmagical form. And so they had pretended to lose their memories along with everyone else. It was easier that way.

"I made you something," Yasmin said, handing Alex the paper bag in her hands. "Hope you like it."

"Thanks," Alex said, touched. He felt bad that he didn't have anything to give her in return, but he knew that would change soon; he had been saving up for tickets to a Mets game.

Inside the bag was a simple composition book. Yasmin had covered it with pictures of everything that Alex loved: monsters and aliens, creepy clowns and killer dolls, spooky old houses and abandoned amusement parks.

The only thing missing was witches. Alex was okay with that.

"It's sad that you lost all your nightbooks," Yasmin said. "I figured you could write some new stories in this one."

"It's perfect," Alex said, his face growing warm. "It's the nicest gift anyone ever gave me."

"Don't get all mushy," Yasmin said, getting to her feet. "Besides, I didn't come here just for you. Where is she?"

Alex nodded toward a large elm tree.

"Over there in the shade," he said. "I guess after all

those years indoors she still hasn't gotten used to the sun."

Lenore was lying in a comfortable spot at the base of the tree. Yasmin and Alex took turns taking care of her, though they suspected that she was happiest when the three of them were together. The orange cat glanced in their direction now: *I'm glad to see you, but not quite glad enough to walk all the way over there.*

Yasmin checked her watch and gasped in surprise.

"I gotta run," she said. "My parents freak out if I'm like a minute late. Do you really like your present?"

"I love it!"

"Don't just love it," she said. "Use it."

After Yasmin and Lenore left, Alex headed home, flipping through his new nightbook. The empty pages brimmed with possibility.

What if . . .

Alex broke into a run. He had an idea for a new story, and he couldn't wait to get home and start writing.

ACKNOWLEDGMENTS

The first draft of *Nightbooks* required my editor, Katherine Tegen, to be even more brilliant than usual. Without her guidance, you would be holding a much different—and inferior—book in your hands. Much gratitude as well to the rest of the amazing team at Katherine Tegen Books! I also want to thank my agent, Alexandra Machinist, whose work ethic and sound judgment never cease to amaze me. Props to Alli Minetti for reading the original manuscript and giving me the perspective of a (crazy smart) fifteen-year-old reader. Thanks to my friend and fellow teacher Lindsay Coral for sharing her knowledge of Syrian culture. Finally, I couldn't have written a single spooky word without the love and support of my wife, Yeeshing, and our three sons: Jack, Logan, and Colin. You are my happily ever after.